"Do beauty and happiness ever last?"

Margot asked the question with a shiver, as she was reminded of the confession she still had to make.

"I don't know. We take them very much for granted, but perhaps we make or mar our own happiness."

"I don't want to do that," she admitted, "but—"

Elliott looked across the table at her as she hesitated. "I can't imagine you making a mistake," he said.

"I've made so many," she said regretfully. "I've been swayed so often by indecision and regret."

"But you've been successful. You surely can't have regrets about your career?"

"That wasn't quite what I meant." And she wondered if she should tell him now who she really was.

Jean S. MacLeod, the author of more than
fifty romance novels, lives with her husband on an
isolated peninsula in Scotland's Western
Highlands. From her doorstep she has a
breathtaking view of the Hebrides. "In these
surroundings," she says, "it must surely be
possible to go on writing for a very long time."
Indeed, her ideas and words are as fresh and
romantic as ever.

Books by Jean S. MacLeod

HARLEQUIN ROMANCE

Shadow on
the Hills

Jean S. MacLeod

Harlequin Books

TORONTO • NEW YORK • LONDON
AMSTERDAM • PARIS • SYDNEY • HAMBURG
STOCKHOLM • ATHENS • TOKYO • MILAN

Original hardcover edition published in 1989
by Mills & Boon Limited

ISBN 0-373-17061-0

Harlequin Romance first edition May 1990

CHAPTER ONE

STANDING above the pass in that vast world of rolling hills and cloud-flecked sky, with the Border country stretched out for miles beneath her, green and peaceful and kind to the eye, Margot Kennedy was instantly aware of an odd feeling of belonging, although she had never been to Scotland before. She had come on an impulse because she had been told by a Harley Street specialist, after a virus infection which had attacked her vocal cords, leaving her with a 'husky throat', that it would be at least a year before she would be able to sing again. Singing was her career, her whole life, and she had wept when she had told her agent that she must refuse the contract he had just gained for her, turning away a golden opportunity which would have sealed her success in the world of music, and Henry Levitt had understood. It had meant so much to her and one small, insignificant bug had changed everything!

'Not for a year,' the specialist had said, and she had accepted his verdict.

'What am I to do?' she had cried to Henry in her desperation. 'What else can I possibly do?'

A whole year. It seemed an eternity as she stood in that high place, contemplating the lonely hills. 'You'll sing again,' Henry had predicted optimistically. 'This isn't for ever. Go away for your year and rest your voice, and I shall keep in touch. Something else will turn up. Leave London,' he had advised. 'You would only fret living here at the hub of things. Find somewhere utterly different where you can look at life from another angle.'

It was then that Scotland had occurred to her. The idea had come out of nowhere, a vague memory of something she had heard in the past connected in her mind with vast open spaces and frowning hills, and overlaid with a suggestion of inadequacy. She stood there, struggling with a name, till she remembered Nigel Grantley, who had spoken often of Scotland because it had been his home.

A shadow swept over the hills, a cloud flying before the boisterous wind which tugged at her hair, leaving its mark on the golden landscape. Nigel had known about disappointment, too, and frustration, and fear that the future could hold nothing for him, and in the end he had given up hope. The thought of his untimely death saddened her as she walked back to the car she had driven from London in two days; there had been no need to hurry such a momentous journey, when it might so easily concern the rest of her life. It all seemed such a ghastly waste. Talent, she thought, was a stern master, and Nigel's talent had demanded too much of him.

The shadow on the hills gave way to brilliant sunshine as she descended into the valley below with Peel Fell behind her and the great Cheviot himself standing in splendid isolation in the east. Two weeks ago she had written to an estate agent in Galashiels suggesting that he might be able to find her a suitable house to rent for at least a year, and the reply she had received from him was at least encouraging.

Her thoughts slipped rapidly away from the past as she approached the lovely old Border town encircled by its shining rivers and guarded by its sheltering fells, convincing herself that she could live quite happily here for the next twelve months, at least. It was no use feeling that she had been cheated in some way; she was being forced to wait.

When she had parked the car, she made her way to

the office of the house agent—a 'factor', she noted as she referred to the heading of the letter she held. She would have to learn these quaint Scottish references if she was going to stay in this lovely, desirable country for any length of time, she mused. 'Involve yourself,' Henry had said. 'Find something to do.'

The office was on the second floor, reached by a narrow stairway from the street below, and before she had gained the half-landing she became aware of a man standing there, waiting for her to come up. Tall, dark and arresting, he seemed to block off the entire staircase, standing with the red-and-white leaded panes of a high, arched window behind him and the sun flooding through to blind her for a moment of hesitation which left them regarding each other uncertainly before he moved aside to let her pass.

'I'm sorry,' she murmured. 'I didn't see you coming down.'

Their eyes held for a moment, his blue and penetrating, hers vaguely bewildered, as she felt that she had seen him somewhere before.

'It's a narrow stairway,' he acknowledged. 'Not much room to manoeuvre, but this is the older part of the town where there wasn't much space to build in those days.'

'I'm looking for Mr Gill of Somerled, Fortune and Gill,' she told him unnecessarily. 'The house agents —or should I remember to say "factor"?'

He smiled at the correction, strong white teeth lighting up the darkness of his face.

'It would get you there faster,' he acknowledged. 'Go straight up and it's the door on your left.'

He clattered down the stairs, leaving behind him the faint aroma of good tweed and the suggestion of tremendous strength, which added up to a man of purpose who had a great many things to do apart from gossiping with a stranger on a house agent's stairway.

When she reached the first floor, the glass-panelled doors facing her bore the legend 'Wilson, Farmer & Duns, Solicitors & Notaries', which made her wonder if the man she had just encountered might be a solicitor, although he did not look like one. The suggestion of open spaces and wide horizons about him had been compellingly strong, but perhaps that was letting her too vivid imagination run away with her. He could have been Mr Wilson, or Mr Farmer, or even Mr Duns!

Confusingly aware that she could remember every detail of his appearance, from the strong, dark hair growing thickly above the high brow and the determined jaw and high-bridged nose, to the mouth that could have been kinder had it not been clamped into a hard line of resolution to match the expression in those compelling blue eyes.

The left-hand door at the end of the landing bore the legend she was looking for, and she opened it and went in to be greeted by a red-haired girl in a tweed skirt and matching jumper.

'Can I help you?' the girl asked shyly.

'I have this letter from Mr Gill.' Margot proffered the communication she had received from the agent two days ago. 'I'm looking for a house to let for a short time.'

'Oh, yes. Will you come this way, please?' The girl moved towards an inner glass door. 'Mr Gill is expecting you.'

A small, stout man with a bright red complexion rose from a chair behind the desk in the inner room as they went through.

'Miss Kennedy?' he suggested, even before his letter was placed on the desk. 'I hope you have had a pleasant journey north.'

'Very pleasant,' Margot assured him, sitting down on the chair he had drawn forward for her, 'especially after I crossed the border. I had no idea Scotland would be like this.'

'Your first visit?' Fair eyebrows shot up. 'We must make it memorable for you, in that case.' He glanced at the letter on the desk in front of him. 'I understand that you want to rent a house rather than buy one. That won't be so easy, I'm afraid, but we will do what we can for you. Have you any preferences?'

'Not really,' Margot decided. 'Just—somewhere near here, somewhere among the hills.'

He smiled indulgently.

'You have come to the right place,' he said, 'but I think you already know that. We are surrounded by hills and many rivers, and the dales are full of history. But I am letting my enthusiasm run away with me!' He picked up a bulky folder. 'I'm sure we can find something to suit you.'

He leafed through the copious file, pulling out a photograph here and there attached to the description of the property on offer.

'How big would you want the house to be?' he asked after a moment. 'A cottage or a mansion?'

Margot smiled.

'Certainly not a mansion, Mr Gill,' she assured him. 'I have been ill and I need to rest my voice for a while. I am a singer. I had thought of Peebles—of going to the Hydro for a few weeks—but now my plans have changed. I need a home.' Her eyes clouded over with disturbing memories. 'I want to establish some sort of base for my family, and my father will be joining me as soon as I can find a suitable house. Even if I couldn't be here all the time,' she added on a note of caution, 'I'd like a sort of permanent base for at least three years.'

He passed over a selection of leaflets, commenting

on them one by one. 'A pleasant house, but much too big, I think . . . Just a little remote, I would say . . . Needing a lot of attention, I'm afraid.'

Margot's heart began to sink. Was there nothing for her here, nothing at all?

'I thought it would be easy,' she confessed, 'but now I am beginning to understand.'

He noticed her obvious disappointment.

'Ah,' he said, 'wait a minute! There's Ottershaws. It has just come on to the market. It isn't a big house and there's a handy little village nearby and several farms. It's in an ideal setting, with the Gala Water flowing past and the Tweed virtually on its doorstep.'

'I can see you're a fisherman!' Margot smiled.

'Who wouldn't be in a place like this?' He smiled back. 'It is my great hobby. Does it interest you, Miss Kennedy?'

'I've never tried,' Margot had to confess, 'but my father will appreciate it, I'm sure. Can you tell me something more about Ottershaws?'

'It has always been a family home until recently,' he explained, 'but now it seems to be too big for Elliott to manage on his own.'

She was immediately interested.

'You know it well?'

'Hereabouts, Miss Kennedy, most houses are known and all the local families. As a matter of fact, the owner of Ottershaws has just been in here, offering the house for rent on a long lease, and it would be ideal, it seems. Unfortunately,' he added, 'I haven't had time to write up an adequate description of it or obtain a photograph.'

'When can I see it?' Margot asked.

'Any time.' He looked at her uncertainly for a moment. 'Mr Dundass will be going straight back there. He has a farm to run. Shall I make an appointment for you for tomorrow morning?' he added, pen poised over the desk diary in front of him.

'Yes, please do,' Margot heard herself saying, absurdly convinced that Ottershaws was to be her future home. 'Even without seeing it, Mr Gill, I'm sure it's going to be just right for me.'

'The more I think of it,' he said, scratching his head, 'the more I feel certain. You see, there isn't much else on our books in that line—not for rent.'

She rose to go.

'I must fix up an hotel room,' she told him. 'Where would you recommend?'

'We have several good hotels, most of them central. Try the Golden Hind,' he advised. 'It isn't a busy time at present and I'm sure they will be able to fix you up. I hope you will stay with us,' he added sincerely as he rose to shake her by the hand. 'We'd like to have you hereabouts.'

Touched by his genuine warmth, she promised to telephone from the hotel later on that day.

'I'll get on to Ottershaws right away,' he told her, 'and fix a time for tomorrow. Mr Dundass should be back there within the hour.'

Margot went down the narrow staircase in a vague sort of dream, feeling that her future home had to be Ottershaws. Normally practical enough, she could not account for the strong feeling that the house had been there, waiting for her, especially when it had come on the market just when she needed it, although this could be wishful thinking. The name itself fascinated her, and the fact that it had recently been a beloved home made it more desirable still. It was what she wanted most, a home that would be completely her own. She had enough money to look after it, even though it might have been neglected a little, which was all thanks to Henry Levitt and a successful start to her career.

Turning away from the knowledge that all this was now in the melting-pot, that her career was at a standstill for up to a year, she sought out the hotel the estate agent had recommended, finding it suitably placed near the centre of the town with a solid stone front to it and a revolving door leading on to a spacious hall, where she was soon signing in at the reception desk, having obtained a comfortable room with bath for the night, which she considered would be all she would need.

So, what to do with the rest of the day? She had the car, and her first impulse was to see more of the surrounding countryside or even to try to find Ottershaws for herself, but perhaps that wouldn't be wise, since Mr Gill already had the matter in hand. There might even be someone else interested in the house. Oh, I hope not, she thought, fully convinced now that Ottershaws was her own. More practically, of course, she didn't know exactly where it was!

Motoring away from the town itself, she was utterly enchanted by what she saw. The southern uplands of Scotland seemed to hold out their arms to her, welcoming her to their grassy heart, and over and over again she was bewitched by a view or a sudden bright stretch of water nestling in a sheltered dale. Great rivers poured down from the hills, gleaming in the sunlight as they wound their way to the distant sea, while far to the north there were other hills, the Moorfoot and the Pentlands closing in to shield the silent valleys from the vagaries of the cold north wind. Trees were everywhere, ancient oaks and newly planted firs, but the lasting impression was of singing water shining in the sun and a greenness everywhere she looked. How different, she thought, how utterly different! It was everything that Henry had advised. 'Get away,' he had said. 'Find somewhere utterly different where you can look at life from another angle.'

When she returned to the hotel it was time to phone the agency.

'Mr Gill has fixed your appointment for eleven o'clock tomorrow morning,' she was told. 'We've made a little route map for you and I'll pass it into the hotel on my way home,' the red-haired girl added. 'Ottershaws isn't very far out of town, but you might find it a bit difficult getting there if you don't know the way.'

Everyone was being helpful, Margot thought, and no complications had been mentioned up to date.

Feeling restless, she walked about the town for an hour, getting her bearings, and when she returned to the hotel the promised route map was waiting for her. Studying it carefully after a lavish dinner of poached salmon with hollandaise sauce and a generous helping of pudding, she saw that she had only a short distance to go before she would come to Ottershaws, which made it more desirable than ever, because she did not want to bury herself completely in an isolated property too far off the beaten track where there would be very little life at all.

When dawn broke, with the sounds of activity drifting up to her from the street below, she lay on her bed watching the wavering pattern of sunlight moving across the ceiling until it was time to get up. This new day might be the beginning of a new life for her, if this husky voice was all that was to be left to her of her singing career.

Leaving herself plenty of time to get there, she set off to find Ottershaws shortly after ten o'clock. With a substantial breakfast inside her of porridge, bacon, eggs and mushrooms, accompanied by bannocks and home-made marmalade, she decided that she had no room for eleven o'clock coffee before she reached her destination. Everything was lavish in this amazing country, she thought; even the hospitality.

Studying the route map, she drove along a secondary road under the leafy shade of giant beeches until it began to climb towards the hills, and presently her view broadened into a glorious panorama of hill and sky and cascading river, and she knew that she must be almost at her destination. Small groups of houses appeared by the roadside, built of warm grey stone with low, grey-slated roofs which the weather had mellowed over many years, and very soon she was driving through a village which only seemed to have one main street because a noisy river gurgled pleasantly on the other side. She saw a post office which was also a grocery store, and a larger, stone-built house at the far end of the village, but she knew it couldn't be Ottershaws. It looked aloof and unfriendly, shut away behind an overgrown laurel hedge, hiding its windows as she passed. A boy swung out of a side track on a bicycle and she slowed down to question him.

'Please can you tell me where I will find Ottershaws?'

'Yes.' He paused to scrutinise her, the stranger in their midst. 'You'll go straight on, past that little wood there. You can't miss it. It's the first turning on your left. About a mile. You'll see the gates.' He sat astride the saddle, watching as she drove away.

Conscious of her quickening heartbeat, Margot drove slowly. She was nearly there and it was not quite eleven o'clock. If Mr Dundass was working in the vicinity, he might not even be there yet.

When she came to the high, wrought-iron gates, they were open, as if she was expected—as of course she would be, for an appointment had been made. But there was something very welcoming about the open gates, for all that.

A wide drive went up under trees, ancient beeches

which must have stood there for many years, sheltering the house, with a drift of yellow daffodils lighting the way. Ottershaws itself stood high on a narrow ledge overlooking the valley below. It was an old house, built of stone, with crow-stepped gables and a solid-looking slated roof between the tall chimneys on either side. As she approached it, the sun caught the windows of the upper storey in a noose of light, flashing another welcome.

Parking the car to one side, she approached the massive front door, hesitating for a moment before she rang the bell. There was no response. Quickly she glanced at her watch. It was ten minutes past eleven. She rang the bell again as a yellow Labrador came bounding round the end of the house, followed by a tall man, in knee-breeches and a green Barbour, whom she had seen before. It was the man she had met on the stairway leading to the factor's office the day before.

As their eyes met for the second time, she felt the colour rushing to her cheeks for no known reason, and she tried to laugh her confusion away.

'I wasn't quite sure,' she said. 'I thought I had made a fruitless journey.'

He glanced at his watch.

'Which means I should apologise for being late.' He did not return her smile. 'I'm sorry,' he added, 'but I had other things to do.'

'We've met,' she reminded him. 'Yesterday in Galashiels. You were coming from Mr Gill's office as I went up. Quite a coincidence,' she offered.

'You must want to look over the house,' he suggested, taking a key from his pocket. 'Or have you already made up your mind about Ottershaws? It's somewhat off the beaten track.'

She had already made up her mind, although not in the way he had suggested.

'At the moment,' she said, 'it seems just perfect. I could hardly have imagined such a wonderful view.' Looking back from the top step, she saw the sunlit dale with a broad river running through it and the sweep of green foothills reaching for the higher hills on its far side. 'It's what I had thought about,' she confessed.

'Better come inside,' he advised. 'You won't be living on a view.'

Instantly she thought that he didn't want her to rent Ottershaws, but that was ridiculous, since he had already advertised it.

'The accommodation seems to be just right,' she said, following him into a spacious panelled hall from which a curving staircase led to the upper floor. 'Mr Gill said there were five bedrooms, which will be more than enough for us.'

The Labrador had followed them in, crossing immediately to a closed door where he stood expectantly, wagging his tail.

'Telfer thinks he is coming home,' Elliott Dundass explained. 'He hasn't quite come to terms with living on a farm surrounded by working dogs. This is the study.' He opened the door. 'I used it as an office for some time, but it can easily be converted back to its original purpose. It is, I suppose, the warmest room in the house because it is smaller than the others and faces south.'

It was a lovely room, with a recessed stone fireplace where logs would burn warmly in the iron fire-basket and the sun would pour in through the two high windows facing the spectacular view across the valley.

'I can see my father using this room all the time,' she said spontaneously. 'He will probably need somewhere to be alone.'

Elliott Dundass was still at the door, waiting for

her to move on.

'You'll want to see the rest of the house.'

Suddenly she knew that the whole thing was utterly distasteful to him, having to convince a complete stranger that she should occupy a place which had once been his cherished home. She felt it very strongly as they passed from room to room without his making any attempt at trivial conversation as he might have done. He was there to show her round, and that was all.

'I won't take up any more of your time,' she told him half an hour later as they descended the staircase after an inspection of the bedrooms. 'It won't really be necessary. I've seen all I want to see, Mr Dundass, and——'

'You're not impressed?' he suggested, the penetrating blue eyes holding her gaze without flinching. 'It may be too big for you, unless, of course, you are married with a family. It's a grand place for a child,' he added almost reluctantly, the indifference fading from his eyes.

'I'm not married.' She hesitated. 'But there is a child. I shall be bringing her to Scotland with my father as soon as I can settle in. I've put it all very badly, Mr Dundass,' she added. 'I'd love to take Ottershaws and—and look after it. I must have fallen in love with it as soon as I saw it through the trees.'

He turned away.

'I'm glad of that,' he said unexpectedly. 'It's a house that needs to be lived in.'

'I know what you mean. Like Mary Rose's island that "liked to be visited"!' She turned back to look into the long drawing-room shrouded in dust-sheets. 'It will soon come to life again, I promise you.'

Their eyes met, and she knew that she was instantly attracted to this tall, gaunt man who exuded such strength of purpose yet also seemed vulnerable

in an odd sort of way. The impression that they had
met before assailed her again, as it had done the day
before on the narrow stairway leading to the factor's
office, but Elliott Dundass was already at the door,
expecting no more questions. Carefully he locked it
behind them.

'Perhaps you would like to see the gardens,' he
said.

'Do you have the time to show me round?'

He shrugged.

'I wouldn't expect you to rent the house without
taking its surroundings into consideration,' he told
her. 'There's quite a bit of land and several
outbuildings to look after.'

Margot fell into step beside him, the Labrador
bounding joyously ahead of them to show the way
round the gable end of the house into a walled
courtyard flanked by stone buildings, where a Range
Rover stood waiting. Elliott Dundass had obviously
parked it there before he had walked round to the
front of the house to meet her.

'It's larger than I thought,' she confessed, 'but
adequate. I'll have garaging for my car and perhaps
stabling for a pony in time.'

With a little more enthusiasm, he led her towards
the stable block.

'I'll clean it out for you,' he offered, 'before you
move in.'

At last she felt herself accepted, although there was
still that odd sense of some kind of barrier between
them which she might be able to surmount in time.

'Where will you live?' she asked as they walked
back towards the front of the house to enjoy the
spectacular view. 'Do you mean to leave the district?'

'Heavens, no!' he said. 'I have a farm to run up
there on the hill.' He indicated the green pastures

on the other side of a small wood. 'It's the sort of life
that keeps you busy twenty hours of the day.'

Wondering if that was dismissal, if Ottershaws and
the farm on the hill were not to be considered as one
in any sense of the word, she held out her hand.

'Thank you for showing me over your home,' she
said. 'I've fallen in love with Ottershaws and I'll do
my best to keep it just as it is.'

He looked down into her eyes.

'I believe you will,' he said after the barest
hesitation. 'Thank you.'

He held her car door open for her to get in and she
drove away, aware of him standing there in front of
his ancient home with the sun full on his face until
she had disappeared from view. How long he would
remain there she did not know, but she thought that
he no longer resented her intrusion and was glad.

He had let her go without suggesting that they
might meet again, a man with his own interests and
his own set of values, a man not to be easily
forgotten, but surely in the ordinary way of things
they would inevitably stumble across each other, if
only to say hello?

The following morning she returned to the factor's
office to confirm their bargain, and was met by a
beaming Mr Gill and a drawn-up contract.

'I thought you would find Ottershaws to your
liking,' he remarked, 'so I took the liberty of
preparing this for you to sign after I had phoned Mr
Dundass.' He sat with his pen poised over the legal
document on the desk before him. 'It just remains for
me to fill in the period of time. You did say around
three years, Miss Kennedy?'

She nodded. 'What did Mr Dundass feel about
such a long lease?' she asked curiously.

'He was probably quite relieved.' The factor slid the
document across the desk. 'No one wants a house to

stand empty for any length of time these days.'

'He hadn't thought of selling it?'

'No.' He put two little crosses on the document. 'If you will just sign here and here, I'll get Mr Dundass to sign his portion and forward it to you in London.'

'You have my address,' she said as they shook hands. 'I'd like to move in as soon as possible.'

'I'll look forward to seeing you again when you can call in for the keys, and I hope you'll be very happy among us for the next three years,' he said.

'I feel sure I will be,' she assured him. 'I may not be here all the time, Mr Gill, but my father will be. He is a great fisherman.'

'He couldn't have come to a better place!' The little man's eyes gleamed. 'You have the Gala Water right on your doorstep and the Tweed only a stone's throw away, as I told you, to say nothing of the Yarrow and the Ettrick rushing down from the hills. It's a fisherman's paradise and I wish you joy of it, Miss Kennedy. You'll make friends here, I can assure you.'

Margot went down the narrow staircase wondering if the first seeds of a friendship had already been sown, yet she could not think of Elliott Dundass rushing into one immediately with a stranger in their midst. He would take his time to assess her and all she might do or not do for Ottershaws. Besides which, she reminded herself, he was probably a very busy man with a sheep farm to attend to, and much else besides.

She looked out towards the surrounding hills as she walked slowly back to the hotel to pack her case for her return to London. It was a different life altogether and one which had already begun to stir her pulses in anticipation of a new beginning. 'You'll make friends here, I can assure you,' the jolly little factor had said.

Loitering in the main street, she looked at the shops, admiring the colourful local tweeds and the beautiful handmade shoes. I'll need some of these, she thought, a whole new wardrobe so that I can climb the hills and walk along the winding road beside the river without being hampered by high-heeled shoes. A change for you, Margot Kennedy, she mused, but a delightful one in many ways. When her father and Amy were established at Ottershaws her life would be almost complete.

Almost? For a moment the thought of her arrested career was uppermost in her mind, until she brushed it resolutely aside. Looking back and saying 'if only' never solved anything.

When she finally reached the hotel she decided that she had time for a coffee before she packed her small travelling-case and set out on her journey south. The hotel appeared to be empty at such an early hour, but she supposed there would be a bell somewhere which she could ring for service. She crossed the deserted entrance hall where she had booked in the day before, hesitating at the double glass doors opening into the residents' lounge which also seemed to be deserted, but since the doors were wide open she went in to search for the necessary bell.

Barely inside the long, sunlit room, she was suddenly frozen in her tracks by the sound of a girl's high-pitched voice rising in wildly accusing protest.

'You must go in search of her, Elliott. You must find her and punish her for what she has done!'

In that split second Margot had recognised Elliott Dundass standing by the fireplace with his back to her and facing a young girl in a tartan skirt and a practical-looking Barbour, a lovely girl with auburn hair flowing over her shoulders and a small, oval face marred only by the expression of passionate anger which disfigured it.

'It will take time, but I will go, sooner or later,' Elliott Dundass agreed.

Margot heard the now-familiar voice, firm and accusing, as she stood there, unable to move. She had stumbled upon something so intimate that she found herself wishing that the ground would open and swallow her up.

'Sooner or later?' The girl's passionate, almost childish tones rose in a crescendo of accusation, filling the room with insistence. 'You can't leave this till later, Elliott—you know you can't. It's now you have to think about—doing it now. You vowed to seek her out, remember? You promised me you would!'

Before Margot could turn away Elliott Dundass saw her. He had turned from his companion towards the door, his face suffused with anger, his blue eyes as cold as steel.

'Leave it, Cathy,' he said. 'You have my word, remember?'

Margot hesitated. 'Hello!' she said uncomfortably. 'I was looking for a bell to ring. There seems to be no one around and I was looking for a cup of coffee.'

She could see that they had been served with coffee, the silver tray on the table between them.

'There's bound to be someone around.' He pressed a bell by the side of the fireplace. 'I understand they're a bit short-staffed.'

The girl in the Barbour was regarding her suspiciously.

'You're going to introduce me, of course,' she said.

Elliott's grim mouth relaxed as he turned back to Margot.

'This is Cathy Graeme,' he said. 'An old friend. Cathy, Miss Kennedy wants to rent Ottershaws for a while. She has come from London.'

'From London?' Cathy regarded Margot resentfully, as if the very fact that she was from the metropolis prohibited all hope of friendship between them. 'How long do you intend to stay, and why do you want a house like Ottershaws, anyway?'

Margot smiled.

'I hope to stay for three years, on and off,' she answered, aware that she was also confirming her contract with Elliott.

'Oh, a holiday home!' Cathy assumed. 'That won't do a lot for Ottershaws.' She glanced at Elliott. 'I thought you said you wanted someone to take care of the place,' she added bluntly.

Elliott Dundass turned away from the fire.

'I've no doubt Miss Kennedy will do that very well,' he said. 'She seemed—pleased with Ottershaws, and that's as far as we can go, Cathy.'

Margot felt embarrassed. Who was this outspoken girl who apparently had the right to question her future landlord? Someone who had a claim on his affections, perhaps, although she seemed far too immature for such a man.

'Cathy will be your nearest neighbour,' Elliott explained. 'Her people farm across the river from Ottershaws, and she breeds ponies for a living. If you want to ride eventually, I'm sure she will be able to fix you up with a suitable mount.'

'I'd have to learn first,' Margot confessed, 'but the idea sounds attractive since I'll have all the time in the world on my hands once I come up here. By the way,' she added as Cathy marched towards the door, swinging her shoulder-bag over her arm in frank dismissal, 'I've signed my part of the contract with Mr Gill—for three years.'

He looked faintly surprised.

'You're in a hurry to get here.'

'Once I've made a decision,' Margot said, 'I've never thought there was much point in beating about the bush.'

His mouth curved in a one-sided smile.

'I'll sign my half of the bargain before I go back to Sun Hill,' he promised.

'Sun Hill?' she repeated. 'What a lovely name—and so evocative of a house high on a hillside!'

'It's high enough,' he agreed laconically, 'and windy enough. You can see it from Ottershaws once you know where to look.'

'Elliott,' Cathy Graeme put in determinedly, 'I'm running late. I have to go.'

'Of course. I'm sorry.' He held out his hand to Margot. 'I hope you'll be happy here, Miss Kennedy. It's a grand place, especially for children.'

Cathy pricked up her ears, a questioning frown between her brows, but for once she made no comment. Instead she looked Margot over with renewed criticism as she held out her hand.

'Well, goodbye,' she said. 'I hope you'll be happy at Ottershaws, but I doubt it.'

A strange beginning to her new life, Margot thought as she watched them go—and to what might have proved a worthwhile friendship.

CHAPTER TWO

A WEEK later Margot was back in Scotland, having sold the flat she had shared with her father for the past two years. They had been happy enough in Clapham in one half of an old Edwardian house near the Common, but recently she had sensed a restlessness in him which she could quite understand. A man of action all his life, he had never been able to settle anywhere after her mother's death, but Amy had been the complication which had kept him in England for the past four years, Amy and the hope that one day he would see her settled in a more stable situation than a London flat.

Well, now they were ready to settle down in Scotland, Margot thought, driving through Galashiels, where she had picked up the keys to Ottershaws. In a matter of days Amy would be free to wander at will in a Scottish garden, with a gurgling river at their front door and the freedom of the hills all about them. As for her own reaction, she had put the immediate future firmly behind her, willing to spend a year in the wilderness to protect her voice.

And what a wilderness! She drew in deep breaths of the invigorating Scottish air, knowing herself content for the time being.

There was a lot to do at Ottershaws. It had been unlived in for many months, tended once a week by a village woman who had come in to dust, considering that was all that was necessary when no one lived there. Margot met her on the second day after she arrived with a car-load of personal possessions which she had brought with her and was happily distri-

buting around the house when the back door
opened.

'I heard you had arrived,' Elspeth Daley said,
eyeing her with frank curiosity, 'and I was
wondering if you would need my help now that you
have taken over the house. I've been coming here all
my working life,' she added pointedly, 'both before
and after my marriage.'

Margot considered the point.

'I will need someone,' she decided carefully. 'Were
you Mr Dundass's housekeeper?'

'These past two years.' Elspeth Daley drew her
hand across the top of the dresser and examined her
fingertips. 'You've been dusting,' she observed.
'There's not much need for that every day up here
among the hills. Things don't get dusty when you're
away from the main road.'

Margot smiled.

'It's become a habit with me, Mrs Daley,' she
confessed. 'What I was really thinking about was
cooking and that sort of thing. I'm not a very good
cook, you see, and my father will be joining me at the
end of the week.'

'I heard there was a child.' Elspeth was being
cautious.

'Oh, yes—Amy, but she won't be any trouble, I can
assure you. She will be my responsibility.'

'Is she at the school?' was the next enquiry.

'Not yet. She's just four, but I'd like her to go to the
local school when she's five.'

Elspeth was obviously surprised.

'There's a good one in the village, but I
thought——'

'I wouldn't send her away to school, if that's what
you were going to say,' Margot answered. 'She
needs a home atmosphere, and that's what I intend
to provide.'

Elliott Dundass's ex-housekeeper stood looking at her.

'Well,' she said, at last, 'is it yes or no?'

'I'm sure it's yes, Mrs Daley, since you must know the house very well,' Margot decided.

'I can't live in. I have my own family to see to, but if there was an emergency I dare say I could manage the odd night or two.' Elspeth stood waiting, hands on her ample hips.

'That's very good of you, Mrs Daley,' Margot acknowledged. 'I know your family has to come first, but if I had to go back to London for a few days, it would be reassuring to know you were in command.'

They smiled at each other.

'Well, that's all right, then,' Elspeth said. 'It suits both of us. When would you like me to start?'

'Right away, if you can manage it.'

'I'll be here tomorrow morning.'

Watching her go, Margot felt relieved. This was someone who knew Ottershaws, someone who had helped care for it in the past. Mrs Daley, the daily! What could be more suitable?

Footsteps on the paved area outside took her to the back door. Perhaps Elspeth had forgotten something. When she opened the door, Elliott Dundass was standing there.

'Oh—come in!' She stood back, feeling a telltale colour rising in her cheeks as she wondered why he had come. 'I've just had a visit from Mrs Daley. She's promised to work for me.'

He stood in the centre of the kitchen floor, seeming to fill the whole room with his presence.

'I came to deliver these.' He put a set of keys on the table. 'They're a spare set. I thought you might need them.'

'Yes—thank you.' She picked up the keys. 'They'll be handy when my father gets here at the weekend.'

He stood looking at her for a moment, until his gaze went beyond her to the little personal things she had done to the big family kitchen where he must have spent many happy hours as a child.

'I thought you might be one of those people who would want Ottershaws merely as a holiday house,' he said.

She shook her head.

'On the contrary,' she said, 'it will be our home as soon as we get settled in.' When he seemed to be waiting for an explanation, she offered it willingly. 'I've had quite a winter,' she explained. 'I've been ill for almost three months with a throat infection, and London is no place to recuperate. I caught some sort of virus—some bug or other which they don't seem to know very much about—and it settled in my throat. Hence the husky voice!'

'I thought it most attractive,' he said, and she believed him because he didn't seem the sort of man who would pay an idle compliment just for the sake of conversation. 'Our Border air will soon put that right.'

'It's working already,' she told him. 'I feel able to breathe freely after only two days here.' She hesitated. 'I haven't changed very much in the house,' she went on to assure him. 'I'd like to keep it just as it is.'

'You are free to change anything you want,' he said slowly. 'You will be living here now, not me.'

If there was regret in his eyes, she didn't see it because he had turned his head away.

'Would you—like to look over the house now that I've moved a few things?' she suggested.

'There's no need,' he said. 'By the way, I'm glad Elspeth has agreed to stay with you. She has worked here for a long time.'

'Is she a "treasure"?' Margot asked, warming to

this show of friendliness. 'I really do need one.'

'I wouldn't call her that, exactly.' He smiled for the first time. 'But she does know Ottershaws and loves it. She will tell you all you need to know,' he added with a bluntness she had come to expect of him, 'but she won't gossip about you in the village. It's a sort of recognised thing as far as she's concerned—a kind of loyalty.'

'I'll be grateful for that,' Margot assured him, walking with him to the door. 'Not that I have anything to hide!'

Out in the sunshine, he stood to look at the garden.

'It's got out of hand,' he admitted. 'A farmer should never undertake the upkeep of a garden when he's got sheep on the hill. I'll send someone down to help till you've got straightened out.'

'There's rather a lot of it,' she acknowledged.

'Three acres. It's mostly woodland, of course.' He looked out at his former domain. 'You'll find a stream down there and "a host of golden daffodils".'

'I've already seen them.' She closed the back door behind her. 'When Mrs Daley appeared I was going down there to pick some for the house.'

He walked with her along the unkempt path.

'This used to be a tennis court.' He halted at the stretch of grass beyond the lawn. 'It might be useful to you in the summer and the net is still in the outhouse, I expect.'

'It's like walking into an Aladdin's cave,' she suggested, 'finding all these unexpected things!'

'I'm sure you'll make good use of them.'

There was a little gate at the side of the lawn which led to a rough track going down to the village, and with an odd sense of disappointment she thought that they had come to the parting of their ways.

'I was going to ask you about the wood,' she began. 'Whether it was safe for a child to go there on her own.'

They passed the gate.

'Perfectly safe,' he assured her. 'It's part of the Ottershaws' policies.'

She looked at him uncertainly for a moment, and then she laughed.

'Is that another Scottish word I have to learn?' she asked. 'I stumbled on "factor" the day we met that first time at the agent's office.'

'It won't be long before you start using them yourself,' he promised. 'A "policy" hereabouts is what you would call an estate.'

They had reached the edge of the wood, where she held her breath at the sight of a sea of daffodils moving gently in the wind. From the distance of the house they had looked lovely enough, but here, close at hand, they were like bright yellow lamps, their golden trumpets reflecting back the sun.

'I must gather some,' she said spontaneously. 'Ever since I was a child I've loved them, and they'll lighten up the house. I can see a bowl of them against that lovely mahogany panelling in the dining-room, can't you?'

She was immediately sorry as the question left her lips, because his eyes clouded at a memory and his jaw was suddenly tensed.

'I'm sorry,' she apologised quietly. 'I—shouldn't have reminded you.'

'I've got to get used to that,' he said. 'You did nothing wrong.'

Stooping, he helped her to gather the flowers until she had a whole armful of them.

'They've grown here for as long as I can remember,' he told her. 'They were always the first sign of spring after the snowdrops had died. My mother used to watch for them from her window.' They turned back towards the house. 'She was a great gardener,' he added when they came to the formal rosebeds. 'She loved roses and I've tried my hand at pruning these, but I haven't the necessary green fingers.'

'Nor have I,' Margot acknowledged, 'but I'm sure they will survive till my father gets here. He's the expert, but he might need a little help.' She hesitated. 'Perhaps there's someone in the village you can recommend?'

'Alex Whitelaw might help,' he decided. 'I dare say he would come up one day a week, to oblige, you understand!'

Their eyes met, grey on blue, as she felt a new warmth stealing over her.

'I get the message!' she acknowledged. 'And now can I offer you some coffee? I'll be making some for myself before I start to arrange the daffodils,' she added eagerly.

Too eagerly, apparently, when she saw him hesitate.

'Perhaps some other time,' he said. 'It hasn't taken you long to establish yourself, and you'll be here for most of the summer, I suppose.'

'For longer than that,' she found herself assuring him. 'I think I'm almost looking forward to long winter evenings getting to grips with all these books of yours.' Once again she was touching on the past, knowing how much it had meant to him, but it was something they could hardly avoid in the circumstances, and perhaps if they could talk about it more fully some day she would not feel so guilty of intrusion. 'I've brought a few books of my own,' she added, 'and I'd like to buy more, if only to get to grips with the wonderful history of the Borders.'

'You'll find all you need in the library,' he told her. 'Walter Scott and a host of others who have chronicled the past and made it live for us. Try the

Border Reivers for a start,' he smiled. 'We were a wild lot in those days!'

'I feel I have been warned!' She walked with him round the gable end of the house. 'Is there anything else I should know?'

He looked down at her with a smile in his eyes which lightened them like sunlight in dark places.

'Nothing for the present,' he said. 'You seem to be doing pretty well as it is.'

'I've thought about somewhere like Ottershaws for a very long time,' she confessed, 'because I suppose what I wanted more than anything else was a family home.'

He didn't answer that, and when she turned to look at him his whole face had changed, his blue eyes suddenly dark again with remembered pain.

'Ottershaws has always been a family home until recently,' he said, the cold reserve back in his voice. 'Perhaps I should never have parted with it, even for a year or two; perhaps I should have married and settled down here, as I was meant to do, and brought up a family, but that has proved impossible. My brother was killed in an accident just over a month ago,' he added, 'and that made a difference. There were too many memories for me here.' He turned away. 'And a lot of questions I have to ask before I can organise my own life and think about the future,' he added slowly. 'For the moment I'm running the farm up there on the hill which should have been my brother's, and I have very little time to spare for—other things.'

The tight mouth and steely eyes made a different man of him, Margot thought, feeling shut out as he thanked her for the offer of the coffee and went away.

For the next hour she busied herself around the house, arranging the armful of daffodils he had helped her to pick. The library was the room she would use most, she decided, because it was smaller than the others, with a wide view over the river to the undulating hills in the north, and she would probably read a lot in her spare time.

Carrying a blue bowl full of daffodils to place it against the dark panelling, it seemed that she had brought all the April sunshine into the room where she had already set out some of her personal belongings—her writing-compendium, a treasured silver lamp and several photographs of her family taken over the years. There were no photographs of the Dundass family anywhere in the house, she had noticed, not even a portrait, which she thought strange. Turning to the bookshelves, she took down a volume at random, opening it to read the scrawled message on the title page. 'To Neil,' it said, 'from Elliott, his brother.'

Short and concise, it taught her much about the man who had just left Ottershaws to return to his lonely vigil on the hill. Even in his youth, because the unformed handwriting was that of a schoolboy, Elliott Dundass had prized his brother greatly. The bond between them had been very strong, as she discovered when she found volume after volume similarly signed, always with the native reserve of the Scottish male, but telling for all that, and always to 'my brother, Neil'.

As she replaced the last book, she was suddenly conscious of being watched, and when she turned to the open door Cathy Graeme was standing there looking at her.

'I didn't expect you to take possession quite so soon,' she observed bluntly and resentfully. 'When I found the back door unlocked, I thought Elspeth Daley was here,' she went on to explain. 'Elliott will be surprised, to say the least.'

Margot smiled at her.

'He's just been here,' she said. 'He came with an extra set of keys.'

The light of resentment grew in Cathy's eyes.

'I wouldn't have thought he had time for visiting, with the lambing just over and the ewes needing a lot of attention,' she observed. 'Did he stay?'

'Not for very long. We had a look at the garden and he told me about his brother.'

'About Neil?' Cathy looked astonished. 'But he wouldn't talk about Neil—not to a stranger,' she declared.

'Perhaps I—jumped the gun a little,' Margot confessed, 'suggesting that Ottershaws was my idea of the perfect family house.'

'Elliott should never have parted with it,' Cathy declared. 'He could have shut it up permanently, or married and settled down here and had a family. The memories would have gone then, in spite of the pain.'

Margot did not want to discuss the past with this tempestuous girl who wore her emotions so obviously on her sleeve.

'It takes time,' she said. 'Time to forget. You must have known Elliott for a long while.'

'All my life,' Cathy informed her, coming to stand in front of the fire. 'We were all brought up together, Elliott, Neil and me. Nothing should have parted us.' Suddenly the bright face was distorted by hatred. 'Neil should never have died so terribly!'

'Elliott said it was an accident,' Margot offered.

Cathy turned to her in anguish.

'It was no accident!' she declared. 'It was brought about by a selfish woman he met in London who brushed him off when—when he told her he loved her, and went on her way without a care.'

'Cathy,' Margot said, 'I'm sorry.'

'Why should you be?' Cathy demanded. 'You are

only a stranger here.'

'I hope I'm not going to be that for very long.'
Margot crossed the hearthrug. 'I'm going to try to fit
in, Cathy, as quickly as I can.'

'You'll never fit in!' Cathy declared emphatically.
'You're here for a reason of your own, and you'll go
off again whenever it suits you.'

Margot met her stormy eyes across the hearth.

'You're wrong,' she told her quietly. 'I've got the
strongest of reasons for wanting to stay. I've a child
to bring up as best I can. My father will be here at the
end of the week, and he is bringing Amy with him. I
know she is going to love Ottershaws and I want her
to be happy.'

'What age is she?' Cathy asked reluctantly.

'Four—going on five.'

'She'll be ready for the village school,' Cathy
pointed out. 'If she has been pampered in the past,
that will be quite a shock for her.'

Margot smiled.

'She has months to settle in,' she pointed out, 'and
all the lovely summer weather to explore the countryside. I'm looking forward to that more than
anything,' she confessed. 'And now—can I offer you
some coffee? I was just about to have my own, but
Elliott refused to stay for a cup.'

Cathy's eyes were searching the familiar room,
looking for something she apparently missed.

'I suppose he has taken all the family photographs
to Sun Hill,' she observed. 'Certainly he wouldn't
leave them with a stranger.'

'No,' Margot agreed, 'perhaps not. Will you have
some coffee, or are you in too great a hurry to get
away?'

Cathy hesitated for only a second.

'I came over on my bike and I have to get back to
see to the ponies. I live with my parents on the farm

over the river,' she explained. 'You can see it from this window, but it's several miles by the road. There's a footbridge, though, and that's why I brought my bike. It's called Lowther Mains. I was born there,' she added briefly.

Margot walked with her to the back door where a ramshackle bicycle was propped against the outside wall.

'You'll come again?' she suggested.

'If I can find the time.'

'I think you'll like Amy.'

'I suppose so. Children are my speciality. I teach them to ride.'

'You have ponies for hire?' Margot was immediately interested. 'But maybe you don't teach children as young as Amy.'

'Four isn't too young,' Cathy decided. 'I learned to ride when I was four.'

'Then——' Tentatively, Margot held out her hand. 'Perhaps we shall meet again quite soon, Cathy. Can I bring Amy over one day to see the ponies?'

Again there was a momentary hesitation before her visitor answered.

'You can bring her if you like, but I shall have to make the final decision,' she stipulated. 'Some children just don't take to horses.'

Away she went, full of her own importance and the unhappy memories she nursed of a first forlorn love-affair. Cathy, strong-willed and emotional, had loved Neil Dundass with a young girl's first great passion, and that was why she was now transferring most of that girlish affection to his brother, Elliott.

Margot went slowly back into the house, closing the door behind her.

The following morning she met Elliott outside the village post office where she had gone to buy stamps. He had collected his mail and a newspaper, and was

about to get into his Range Rover, but he stood
waiting for her to come to the kerb.

'Cathy tells me you are expecting your father
tomorrow,' he said. 'I hope he is going to find everything in order.'

'I'm sure he will,' she answered, thinking how
beautiful the day had become. 'It's a man's country,
isn't it?' she added, looking towards the hills. 'Sheep
and farming—and fishing, perhaps, when you have
time!'

'Time is essential,' he agreed, 'but the worst of the
weather is past and the lambing over, so I've got time
to spare.'

'Do you think——' she began, and then thought
better of the request she had been about to make.

'What did you want me to think about?' he asked,
with the humorous twist of his lips which she was
beginning to recognise. 'Were you going to ask a
favour?'

'Something like that.' She smiled up at him. 'My
father loves to fish, and I wondered if there was anywhere locally where he could spend half a day or so
with the rod he will surely buy as soon as he gets
here.'

'I could easily arrange it,' he agreed, 'as soon as I
get back from London.'

'Oh—you're going off quite soon?' She had tried to
keep her disappointment from showing. 'Well—after
you return, perhaps. I saw Cathy yesterday about
riding lessons for Amy,' she went on quickly. 'She
told me she ran a riding-school, but she wanted
time to consider another pupil. Cathy doesn't expect
me to stay at Ottershaws for very long,' she added
whimsically as their eyes met and held.

'And will you?' he asked, making it sound more
like a challenge than an ordinary, straightforward
question.

'Yes,' she said firmly, 'I mean to stay. Will you come and meet my father?' she added, saying as he hesitated, 'Please come! He's such a man's man, and I feel he's entirely out of his element in a woman-dominated ménage.'

He smiled at the idea and her pulses quickened. This was something else she wanted—his friendship for her father and his understanding of what she was trying to do at Ottershaws. In a handful of meetings she had recognised him as a man she could admire, a man of integrity strong enough to meet any challenge which life might present, a man who would tell the truth whatever it might cost him. A surging feeling suggested that they had been destined to meet, that Elliott Dundass was the embodiment of many of her dreams and much of her need.

Yet, in a curious sort of way, he had already created a barrier between them which she suspected had a great deal to do with what Cathy chose to call 'his pain'. His brother's death had come between them at their very first meeting, but even painful bereavement must pass in the end. She thought about her own brother and how dearly she would love him to return to the family he had spurned when tragedy had laid a cold hand across his heart and they had all been so desperately involved.

And now Elliott was going to London to involve himself even more deeply in his brother's past, seeking to find the woman whose fatal attraction had led to Neil's untimely death.

Cathy Graeme cycled home to Lowther Mains, taking the longer way by the main road and across the three-span bridge where the dark water lay, deep and cool among the rocks. She had a decision to make. If I take Margot Kennedy's daughter, she thought, I'll be forging a link with Ottershaws that I don't really want to make. On the other hand, I need as many pupils as I can get now that the summer is coming on. There are Brown Bess and Pumpkin just eating their heads off in the stables, and they have to be exercised.

She was riding in the middle of the road, pedalling slowly, her brows drawn together in a thoughtful frown, when the Range Rover came towards her, slowing as she would have passed.

'Why the frown?' Elliott Dundass enquired, putting on his brakes. 'You realise, of course, that you are right in the middle of the road?'

'I was trying to make up my mind about something.' Cathy eased herself from the saddle, standing astride the bicycle to look at him. 'Where are you off to?' she demanded. 'Your tenant has taken possession at Ottershaws, so you won't want to go there,' she suggested.

'I'm on my way to Galashiels,' he explained, adding briefly for her further information, 'I was at Ottershaws yesterday to deliver another set of keys in case they would be needed.'

'It's an odd set-up,' Cathy reflected. 'Margot Kennedy and the little girl and her father, but no sign of Mr Kennedy. They say in the village that they must be living apart.'

'The old grapevine!' Elliott smiled after the merest hesitation. 'Who was it this time? The post office or Meg MacPhie?'

'You can scoff,' Cathy accused him, 'but people are bound to be interested when a stranger just appears out of the blue and wants to be taken at face value without divulging anything about herself.'

'Anything sensational, I suppose you mean,' Elliott suggested. 'No, Cathy, I don't think Miss Kennedy is trying to be secretive about her past, or even evasive. She might just not understand about our natural curiosity.'

'She wants me to teach her daughter to ride,' Cathy informed him after a pause.

'There's no reason why you shouldn't,' he pointed out. 'Not with Pumpkin and Brown Bess standing idle down at the Mains.'

'That was what I was thinking about,' she confessed. 'It means the Kennedys will be here most of the summer.'

'Which will be good for Ottershaws,' he decided.

Cathy looked up at him with a world of pity in her eyes, which was a reflection of her own painful loss.

'I know how you must feel about Ottershaws, Elliott—and about Neil,' she acknowledged. 'Going up there must have brought it all back, the terrible sorrow and disappointment and your desire to be avenged.'

It was as if she was determined to remind him of a situation which he might be trying to forget, but there was a new hardness about his mouth when he answered her.

'If it takes me the rest of my life, Cathy, I'll find Olivia Hallam and confront her with the truth.'

'I wish I could go to London with you,' she told him, satisfied that his determination to confront his brother's betrayer was as strong as ever.

'It wouldn't help,' he said, restarting the engine. 'I'll go over Neil's flat and bring the rest of his belongings home.'

'When will you go?'

'Quite soon. I'll have to dispose of the flat.'

'You wouldn't want to keep it on?'

'What would be the point of that?' he said. 'I have no desire to live in London even occasionally.'

'You helped Neil to buy it,' she reminded him.

'Yes, I know, but that was a long time ago.'

She watched him drive away, glad that they still

saw eye to eye about his brother's betrayal and the fact that he was determined to confront Olivia Hallam with her treachery as soon as he reasonably could.

Margot had prepared Ottershaws for her father's arrival, making a special room for Amy overlooking the dale and its surrounding hills where she could watch the grazing sheep on the high pastures and the clouds scudding across the sky to make fleeting patterns on the grassy slopes which seemed to stretch to infinity in this wide Border country where a city child could grow up happily and at peace. Her smile faded when she thought of the little girl so soon to be back with her, and the recurring memory of the past which disturbed her so much. If only James would accept his responsibilities and eventually take Amy to his heart!

A car appeared at the end of the drive, chauffeur-driven, and she ran into the hall, opening the door wide in welcome as she watched an elderly man step out on to the gravel. Tall and distinguished-looking, he walked with the aid of a stick, but otherwise he seemed to be agile enough.

'Margot!' He folded her in his arms. 'How good to be with you again.'

Margot returned his embrace, looking eagerly into the car where a small, shy child was still sitting on the back seat.

'Aren't you coming out?' she smiled. 'This is your new home.'

Amy responded almost reluctantly.

'You said there would be a pony,' she suggested as her feet touched the gravel.

'I've got one in mind,' Margot promised her, kissing her tenderly. 'You will see it tomorrow.'

'What kind of a pony is it?' The light of excitement broke in the solemn brown eyes. 'Has it got a name?'

'I'm not quite sure.' Margot hesitated. 'You see, the lady who owns it only came to see me yesterday, but somehow I think the pony will have a very nice name.'

'Like Whitefoot or Cinders?'

'Could be,' Margot agreed, taking her by the hand, 'and then it could be something quite different, a really Scottish name.'

'Like Porridge,' her father put in, 'or Shortbread!'

'Don't confuse her!' Margot laughed. 'Just pay off your taxi and come in and tell me what you think of Ottershaws.'

He looked about him when the car had driven away.

'You couldn't have made a better choice for your convalescence,' he said, sniffing the keen hill air.

'That wasn't my only reason for coming,' she reminded him.

'No.' He glanced down at the silent child who was now clinging to her hand. 'It will be ideal for Amy in a thousand ways, but—are you sure you want to make this sacrifice?'

'I'm surprised you could think of such a word,' she said quietly, 'especially when you know it won't be that. London was impossible for her, and there was no point in me staying there, either.'

He drew in deep breaths of the cold, invigorating air.

'Good for all of us,' he agreed. 'I was beginning to feel hemmed in down there in London but—this is different.' His keen gaze travelled across the landscape with deep appreciation. 'I've roamed the world,' he admitted, 'without seeing anything better than this. That river down there must be alive with fish or I'm a Dutchman!'

She put an appreciative hand on his arm, leading him towards the house.

'I've a feeling it might be the answer to a lot of things,' she said. 'I'll have to go back to London for a final check-up, but even then I don't suppose I'll be able to use my voice for a long time to come.'

'I'm hungry,' Amy announced.

Margot lifted her over the doorstep, hugging her impulsively.

'Hasn't your grandfather fed you since you left London?' she demanded.

Amy nodded.

'We had our lunch on the train,' she said importantly.

'But now you're hungry again?' Margot laughed. 'Well, Mrs Daley has a wonderful tea ready for you, with a boiled egg and scones and pancakes and—maybe—a cake. We'll go up to your room first, shall we, and unpack your case? Then we can wash our hands and come down for tea.'

Amy regarded her gloved hands for a full minute before she pointed out, 'I washed them on the train. I would rather go and see the pony,' she suggested.

On the way upstairs Margot explained that the pony would be going to bed quite soon and the following day would be a better time to pay it a visit, an explanation which was accepted philosophically enough as Amy inspected her new domain.

'You can have this cupboard for your toys,' Margot suggested, 'when the trunk arrives from London.'

Amy looked worried.

'I think Mr Bear will be glad when he gets here,' she observed. 'It will be dark for him in the trunk.'

'Not too dark,' Margot suggested. 'Besides, bears don't mind. They sleep in the dark all winter.'

Amy's eyes widened.

'This bear doesn't'! He sits on my bed.'

'Of course! I'd forgotten. I was thinking of real live bears.'

'Are there any here, in Scotland?'

'Not now, but there used to be—a very long time ago.'

'I see.' Amy walked towards the door. 'Is it time for tea now?'

Mrs Daley had set the round table in the library with a white, lace-edged cloth and all the home-made delights Margot had promised, even down to a magnificent iced cake which she had produced herself for the occasion. She was instantly delighted by Amy.

'It's nice to have a child about the house again,' she commented. 'Ottershaws has always been a place for children.'

Once their meal was over there was little difficulty in persuading Amy that it was time for bed.

'She'll dream all night about that pony.' Margot smiled when they had settled down in the library where the table had been cleared and a bright log fire burned in the grate. 'I hope Cathy Graeme won't disappoint me,' she added thoughtfully, 'because she really didn't promise anything.'

'And who is Cathy Graeme?' her father asked as he lit his pipe, drawing at it contentedly in the firelight.

'She's the local farmer's daughter from across the river,' Margot explained, 'and she runs a riding-school. I think they breed their own horses, but I can't be sure.'

'Are we going to buy Amy a pony?'

'Not yet. I think she should learn to ride first, and Cathy is the answer.' Margot hesitated. 'It was only that she—didn't seem to be too enthusiastic about taking on another pupil.'

'One more wouldn't make a lot of difference,' her father pointed out. 'If it does, I could teach Amy myself.'

'And fall off a horse again? The answer is no,'

Margot decided. 'You can use the car and go fishing and do lots of other things, but no more horse-riding for the present. You've been around the world so much,' she pointed out almost wistfully, 'but now I hope you are prepared to settle down for a while.'

He regarded her through a haze of tobacco smoke.

'It's something of a curse to have itchy feet,' he admitted, 'but I'll stay for as long as you need me.'

'And then?' she asked anxiously.

'Oh, I'll travel around, writing my books, I suppose.'

She bent towards him.

'Not yet,' she begged. 'Amy needs us both.'

'Yes, I know,' he admitted, 'but she's really her father's responsibility, not mine.'

The smile faded from Margot's eyes.

'One day,' she said hopefully, 'he will come back.'

For a moment he let the silence of the room engulf them.

'We've discussed this so often,' he said at last. 'It's four years now and nothing has changed. You can't compel a man to do something his heart just isn't in,' he added carefully. 'I think we should be realistic about that.'

Margot's eyes dimmed with pain and deep regret.

'I would do anything—anything to get him back,' she said.

'Is that why you rented this place, hoping he would come?' he asked.

'It's part of the reason.' She rose to stand beside the window where dusk was gathering above the hills. 'Amy needs an established home.'

'What about your career?' he asked, the pipe cradled between his hands momentarily forgotten as he bent forward to gaze into the fire.

'I'm not going to think about it for at least six months,' she decided carefully. 'This husky throat is no use to me, and it will only get better if I relax.'

He asked abruptly, because they had always been truthful with each other, 'And if it doesn't?'

'I must find something else to do.'

'It's a terrible waste.'

'I'm not going to think about that.' She turned back to the fire. 'Henry Levitt says there's plenty of time, and I have another appointment with the specialist. I'll see Henry when I go to London and we'll talk,' she decided.

'He's been very good to you.'

'Yes, I know that.'

'Even a bit in love with you.' Her father was smiling now.

'Oh—Henry's half in love with everybody!' Margot declared. 'He'll forget about me in next to no time.'

'Which would be a pity since he's done so much for you already.' Her father shifted his position in the chair. 'Who owns this place?' he asked.

A faint colour stained Margot's cheeks.

'Elliott Dundass. I met him by chance when I first called on the estate agent in Galashiels, and he came here the other day to deliver a second set of keys. I think you'll like him,' she added tentatively. 'He's rather like you.'

'Younger, I hope!' He was watching her closely. 'Is he the local laird?'

'Not quite, but he does own a lot of land, mostly hill-grazing, I think. There's a farm up there somewhere.' She looked up towards the hills. 'It's called Sun Hill and he lives there on his own.'

'Not married?'

'No.'

Used as she was to such playful interrogation, she felt that he was being rather too curious about Elliott Dundass.

'I spoke to him about fishing rights on the river,'

she said, tidying cushions and books before they retired for the night. 'I thought you would like to fish.'

'And what did he say?'

'Oh, it would be all right and he would let you know as soon as he got back from London.'

'Big business?' he asked, knocking out the contents of his pipe in the ashtray she had provided.

'No—no, he's just a farmer. I thought Amy might like to go and see the sheep,' she added quickly. 'The lambing season is just over so there are lots of lambs.'

'She's crazy about animals.'

'Yes, I know. That's why I thought London was so wrong for her.'

He put an arm about her shoulders as they walked towards the door.

'Don't be too sad about coming away,' he said. 'It's going to do us all a world of good.'

She paused when they reached the door.

'Strangely enough,' she admitted, 'I'm not pining overmuch for the bright lights, Dad. I thought I would, but since I've seen Scotland I've changed my mind about a good many things. Henry says my career won't wait too long, but I think it can. I'm looking at this as an interlude, of course, a sort of side road down which I had to go. You'll laugh at that, I know, but it's something I feel very strongly about, and a year isn't a very long time, after all.'

'It can be long enough.'

'You're thinking about James.' She put a hand on his arm. 'I've written and asked him to come here.' Her bright eyes clouded over. 'Do you think he will?'

Her father's mouth tightened.

'I'm not making any predictions,' he said, 'but he's a fool if he doesn't.'

'Amy talks about her father so much.' Margot's tone was wistful. 'It would make such a difference to her. To us all,' she added quietly as they mounted the staircase.

Next morning Amy was up and about before any of them.

'Can we go up there?' she asked, looking out through the dining-room window to the hills. 'Is it very far to walk?'

'We needn't go right to the top,' Margot decided. 'There's sure to be a hill path somewhere leading from the farms.'

'Is that where the lady with the ponies lives?' Amy wanted to know as she sat down to enjoy her first breakfast at Ottershaws.

'No. Cathy lives on the other side of the river with her mother and father,' Margot explained. 'We'll have to wait till she says we can go,' she added as a precaution.

'If she's got lots of ponies, we could just go to *look* at them.'

'We could, but perhaps it would be better to just take a little walk nearer here on this side of the river,' Margot suggested diplomatically. 'To find our bearings,' she added as her father joined them, rubbing his hands together in anticipation as he saw the lavish display of bannocks and home-made preserves Mrs Daley had brought up from her cottage in the village.

'You'll take porridge?' she suggested, placing a steaming bowl of it in front of him before he could refuse. 'And after that there's kippers or ham and egg. You can make your choice.'

'Be warned and don't put sugar on your porridge!' Margot advised under her breath. 'It's next-door to sacrilege in these parts, and the milk comes in a separate bowl to dip your spoon in,' she added with a grin.

'I'm thinking about the kippers,' her father laughed. 'It's a long time since I've had kippers in the morning, but we did have a Scottish housekeeper in Nairobi who had them sent out specially.'

When he had dispensed with the kippers and spread Mrs Daley's homemade marmalade thickly on a bannock, he decided that a walk would do them all good.

'I ought to stay and help with the housework,' Margot reflected, 'but the sun on these hills is a terrible temptation. I can make up for deserting the kitchen later on.'

Mrs Daley saw them off.

'We don't get many days like this,' she informed them, 'so make the most of it. If you keep to that path from the side gate, you'll come on to the hill just short of the wood, then you can walk down to the village by the road.'

Out on the hill, at last, they climbed steadily by what was no more than a sheep track and Amy ran on a little way ahead, almost bewildered by the freedom of it all. The wind in her hair delighted Margot, too, as her father took great gulps of it, striding beside her with a look of contentment in his eyes which she hadn't seen there for a long while. Amy turned back towards them, looking perplexed.

'There's someone coming,' she announced.

Before she could gather her thoughts together, Margot saw Elliott Dundass striding across the heather towards them.

'Does he want us to go away?' Amy whispered.

'No.' Margot drew a deep breath. 'He's just working. Do you see the two dogs? Well, they're gathering in the sheep. Mr Dundass may want them nearer home before he goes to London.'

Elliott came on, the two Border collies waiting for his next command.

'Sit, Nellie!' he ordered. 'Ruff, come in!'

'They must watch the sheep don't scatter,' Margot explained, but already Amy was in a child's wonderland. Gazing in fascination at Nellie, she had eyes for nothing else.

Margot looked up at Elliott.

'I hope we're not trespassing,' she said. 'We didn't see the sheep till we came over the hill.'

'You're at liberty to come and go as you please,' he assured her. 'I was half expecting to see you on such a good day.' He waited for the inevitable introduction.

'This is my father,' Margot said.

The two men shook hands, obviously liking each other.

'And this is Amy.' Margot drew the child forward. 'She loves dogs, but we've never been able to have one because we've always lived in a London flat.'

Elliott signalled to one of the collies to come forward.

'She's quite friendly,' he assured the excited child. 'She won't bite. Would you like to stroke her coat?'

'Oh—please!' Amy reached out to fondle the collie's soft head. 'She's very gentle.'

'She has to be to look after the sheep, especially when they have followers—lambs,' he amended, when Amy seemed puzzled. 'Also she's got four pups of her own to look after.'

Amy's eyes widened.

'Has she left them at home?' she ventured. 'Because they are very small?'

'They're growing fast.' Elliott hesitated for just a moment. 'Would you like to come and see them one day?' he asked.

'Oh!' Amy's eyes shone. 'Yes, please,' she decided.

Elliott looked at Margot.

'You ought to have a dog at Ottershaws,' he suggested.

'But—these are working dogs,' she protested. 'Even the pups must be valuable to you.'

'I think I could spare a pup,' he told her, looking sideways at Amy, who was really too preoccupied to hear.

'She'd love it,' Margot assured him. 'But—you are going to London——'

'There will be someone at Sun Hill to look after the dogs,' he assured her. 'Probably Cathy, who is quite crazy about young animals.' He turned to her father. 'I hear you're a fisherman,' he said. 'There's a stretch of the Gala Water near at hand I can safely recommend. It's full of trout.'

'You're being very accommodating. There's nothing I would like better.'

Margot was well aware of the pleasure her father felt, which left her more grateful than ever to this man who seemed to appreciate Amy's loneliness.

'Are you properly equipped?' he was asking her father. 'If not, I can let you have a spare rod when you come to Sun Hill with Amy. You will also need a net and waders.'

'That won't be any problem!' her father assured him. 'I'll be off to Galashiels tomorrow to get what I need.'

Her father's enthusiasm made Margot smile, although she had noticed that Elliott had not included her specifically in his invitation to Sun Hill, which she longed to see. But there was still Amy.

'Could you come, too?' she asked, tugging at Margot's hand.

Margot met Elliott's gaze, suddenly disconcerted by the expression in his eyes.

'I—Grandpa will help you to choose a pup,' she said uncertainly. 'Mr Dundass has said you can have one.'

'Which means we'll be visiting you tomorrow morning at first light!' Her father smiled.

Elliott nodded.

'Any time after ten o'clock,' he agreed, preparing to go. 'It's the farm up there in the fold of the hills. You can't miss it once you get on to the moor. You'll need strong shoes,' he added. 'The farm track is pretty rough.' This time he was looking at Margot. 'Would you like to come, too?' he asked. 'I dare say I could manage a cup of tea or a glass of milk.'

'The milk will do fine,' she told him, her heart lifting in a ridiculous way because, suddenly, she had been invited to join her family in this first visit to his home among the hills. Not his true home, she supposed, because that would always be Ottershaws, but where he lived his present, lonely existence.

'I'll try to have the house cleaned up before you arrive,' he promised. 'It's got somewhat out of hand lately.'

Which meant that he had no regular housekeeper coming in and very few visitors. Only Cathy, Margot thought, who really wouldn't care too much if the house was untidy or not.

'We'll see you tomorrow,' her father called as he walked away, the collected sheep moving ahead of him with the two dogs at their heels.

Far too early the following morning, Amy was already talking about the journey to Sun Hill.

'It's only eight o'clock,' Margot pointed out, 'and it won't take an hour to get there. Besides, Grandpa hasn't finished his breakfast yet.'

Amy regarded what was left of her soft-boiled egg with a rueful eye.

'I can't eat any more,' she announced.

'No egg, no Sun Hill,' Margot assured her firmly.

'Oh, well——' Amy dug a finger of toast into the neglected egg. 'I wish Grandpa would hurry up with all that shaving he does.'

'He has to be smart to go to Sun Hill.'

'Is that why you're wearing your new skirt?' asked the observant one.

Margot smiled.

'I suppose it is.' She poured herself a second cup of coffee. 'Tell you what,' she added, 'supposing you go out and pick a nice bunch of daffodils to take to Mr Dundass just to say thank you for the puppy.'

Thus encouraged, Amy disappeared for half an hour, returning with a battered bunch of daffodils and bright, rosy cheeks to match her shining eyes. Margot cut the daffodil stems to a fairly uniform length while her father finished his breakfast.

'This pup is going to be utterly spoiled,' he reflected. 'Still, it was nice of Dundass to make the gesture.'

'And kind of him to offer you a rod.' Margot cleared the table. 'I don't suppose he has much time for fishing with so many sheep to attend to.'

'Once a fisherman, always a fisherman!' her father pointed out. 'I've missed it, I must confess. Once you're hooked, you're hooked for life.'

'That sounds more like the fish!' Margot's smile caressed him. 'You may be able to persuade Elliott Dundass to ease up for a day and go out with you, but what I can never understand is the thrill of wading thigh-deep in cold water in order to cast a fly in the right place.'

'Come and watch,' he challenged, 'and then you will understand.'

They reached Sun Hill by a rough farm track that wound gently among the foothills, while all around them sheep with their lambs grazed contentedly in the early sunshine.

'Why do they jump about like that?' Amy wanted to know, watching the group of young lambs gathered in the sunniest spot under a dry stone wall.

'They play a lot, just like you,' her grandfather told her. 'When they're older, they'll get down to the business of eating most of the time.'

Sun Hill was taking up all Margot's attention. It was a small house built of native stone with a grey-slated roof that shone in the sun, and small-paned, deeply recessed windows which would probably make it dim inside, yet it seemed to be engulfed in sunlight, standing as it did near the very crest of a hill. It really did deserve its name, she thought, as Elliott opened the door.

'I hope we're not too early,' she said. 'Amy is most impatient to see the pups.'

'We'll go and have a look at them straight away, in that case,' he said. 'Hello, Amy! Did you see the lambs as you came up?'

He shook hands with her father, leading the way into the house which took them rapidly from sunshine to shade. It was an old farmhouse, low-ceilinged and stone-floored, making no concession to modern living, yet it possessed a charm all its own. When her eyes had fully adjusted to the light, Margot realised that it was very sparsely furnished, with only the necessities a man might need for living. In the long room they entered from the passageway, cured sheepskins covered the floor in front of a vast stone fireplace where a newly lit log fire burned and a low table carved from a tree-trunk stood beside one of only two chairs. Along one wall, a magnificent oak dresser stood patiently, awaiting ornamentation, but in the whole room there was nothing as frivolous as an ornament. Not even a single photograph, Margot observed, remembering that there had been no photographs left behind at Ottershaws either. Elliott evidently wanted to forget the past.

Yet the scene she had witnessed in the hotel lounge when she had unwittingly stumbled upon him with Cathy Graeme did not seem to suggest forgetfulness. 'You must go in search of her, Elliott,' Cathy had cried. 'You must find her and punish her for what she has done!'

And Elliott had answered calmly, 'It will take time, but I will go, sooner or later.'

Was that why he was going to London now, Margot wondered, why he was leaving Sun Hill so early in the year?

Elliott led the way through the small kitchen adjacent to the main living-room to a scullery where the pups were being kept. Nellie had herded her litter of black and white collies into their basket, but as soon as her playful offspring heard their voices they were all over the stone floor, whimpering joyfully at Amy's feet.

'Can I touch them?' she gasped. 'Can I hold one?'

Elliott lifted a squirming pup into her arms.

'There you go!' he said. 'Nellie will keep an eye on you.'

Amy, who had spoken about nothing but Nellie's pups all morning, put down her gift of daffodils on the scullery bench.

'They're for you,' Margot explained. 'I thought you would like some when there are so many at Ottershaws.'

With a man's disregard for such things, he put them into a stone jar standing near the kitchen sink.

'Some of them are slightly tattered,' Margot apologised, 'but Amy was in a hurry.'

He said, 'I'm not sure if there's a vase for you to arrange them properly. There isn't much of that sort of thing here. Only the essentials,' he added as he opened the back door to let in some more light.

'And the view!' Margot drew in a swift, appreciative breath as she gazed down across a wide valley with a broad river running through it and a meandering road wandering by its side. 'It's magnificent!'

'Not too remote, would you think?' he asked tentatively.

'Not at all when there is so much to do,' she answered truthfully.

'You have help, of course?' her father suggested, looking out at a large flock of sheep and their lambs scattered over the hillside.

'A man and a boy—a very old man and a very young boy,' Elliott said, 'but Gavin is willing to learn. Things have changed in the past few years,' he added, leading the way back to the living-room. 'Since my brother left Ottershaws I've had to do without a manager up here. That is why you are at Ottershaws,' he added candidly. 'If everything had gone as we'd hoped, Neil would have been up here now, farming like me.'

Once again Margot was conscious of a remoteness about him which was not too difficult to understand. Up here alone among the hills he would have time to think, to reason and to be his own counsel, and it seemed that his brother's desertion of Ottershaws had hit him hard.

Rather awkwardly he began to make tea, producing three odd cups from a corner cupboard and washing them carefully at the kitchen sink before searching for the necessary saucers.

'There was a tray somewhere,' he reflected as Margot came to the open door. 'I haven't much to offer you apart from a few biscuits Mrs Graeme baked for me last week.'

'Can I help?' Margot suggested, searching in her turn for the elusive tray. 'I could infuse the tea.'

'Thanks,' he said. 'You'll know how your father likes it.'

'Hot and strong and far too sweet!' she laughed, watching her father as he played contentedly with Nellie's pups. 'Amy and my father will never be out of your debt. They both love dogs.'

'I'll train the other three to the hill in time,' he said. 'I don't like to sell a good dog, but four are a bit beyond me at the moment.'

'I can imagine,' she said, still searching for the tray. 'It must take weeks and weeks and endless patience.'

'Obedience is bred in them and they have a sort of instinct for the hill. Nellie has been one of my best dogs so far, and it rubs off on the pups.' He watched as she scalded the teapot. 'I suppose I ought to do that, but it seems a great waste of time,' he observed.

'Not if you like your tea as it should be,' she laughed. 'I'll accept the necessary compliment when you've tasted it!'

'Perhaps you would rather have had coffee?' he suggested.

'No, tea will do fine.'

When they had taken tea, he showed them round the farm.

'There's not much to see apart from the view,' he said.

The farmyard led straight on to the moor, with a few sheep pens in between which he explained were used at the dipping.

'I helped with dipping once, out in Australia,' her father remembered. 'At least, I thought I was being helpful until one of the ewes took exception to my method and pulled me with her through the trough. It was a humbling experience, because I was ready to bet my last dollar that the wretched animal had taken a liking to me!'

'Perhaps you misjudged her strength and her

determination to escape,' Elliott suggested. 'They're never eager to go through the dip, and there's a real knack in handling a struggling one.'

'No use telling her it's necessary and very good for her!'

The two men were getting on wonderfully well, Margot thought, just as she had hoped they would. In no time they were discussing fishing and where her father should go in Galashiels to equip himself for the sport he loved.

'It's five years since I last cast a fly,' he said wistfully. 'I'm eager to get my hand in again.'

Margot walked ahead with Amy, who had been more than reluctant to leave Nellie and the pups behind.

'Can we have one now?' she demanded when they finally turned back towards the house. 'I'd like the littlest one.'

'Mr Dundass will help you to choose,' Margot suggested.

Before they reached the farmhouse door they saw Cathy Graeme coming up the hill, wheeling her bicycle up the final steep gradient, and she looked flushed and angry as they drew near.

'I wanted to use the car,' she said, 'but Father was going to Selkirk to pick up some cattle and I couldn't have it.'

Her explanation was solely for Elliott's benefit, although she finally turned to his visitors with a fixed smile on her lips.

'Hello!' she said, looking directly at Margot. 'I didn't expect to see you here. It's a long way to walk from Ottershaws.'

'We took it in easy stages.' Margot held out her hand. 'Cathy, I'd like you to meet my father. And this is Amy,' she added. 'We came to look at one of Nellie's pups.'

'Oh!' Cathy looked down at Amy, who was sheltering behind Margot's skirts. 'Perhaps you won't want a pony to ride when you have a puppy to look after,' she suggested.

Amy was silent.

'I think we might manage to do both,' her grandfather said, taking the initiative. 'It's quite time Amy knew one end of a horse from the other, and I hear you're the best possible teacher she could have.'

He was at his most engaging, and Cathy succumbed to the twinkling smile in his eyes, albeit reluctantly.

'I'll arrange it,' she agreed, propping the bicycle against the wall of the house as if she meant to stay. 'I've brought some scones for you, Elliott,' she added. 'We baked them this morning.'

Walking past them into the house, she went straight through the scullery to find a tin for her offering, noticing the evidence of the tea-tray beside the sink.

'I'll clear up for you, Elliott,' she offered. 'I know how busy you are, especially in the morning.'

Elliott stood aside for Margot and her father to walk ahead of him into the house.

'I'd like to keep the pup for another day or so,' he said, 'if that won't be too hard on Amy.'

'As long as she knows she can have it eventually, that will be fine.' Margot hesitated at the kitchen door. 'And now we mustn't keep you any longer. I meant to wash up,' she added, 'but you spirited us away to admire your view!'

'Amy has still to choose her pup.' He bent to separate Nellie's squirming offspring. 'How about this one, Amy?' he asked.

'It's got very friendly eyes,' Amy conceded.

'But you'd rather have one of the others,' he guessed, their two heads close together over the basket. 'Perhaps this one, eh?'

'Oh, yes, the littlest one!' Amy agreed.

The sudden rush of emotion which had assailed her so often during the past four years took Margot to the window to hide the tears gathering in her eyes. A man and a trusting child! Amy deserved that, at least.

Cathy was clattering the teacups in the sink, busying herself around the place with a proprietorial air, and it was several minutes before the others joined them.

'I was wondering about a horse to ride,' her father said, waiting for Cathy to turn from the sink. 'I believe your parents breed them down at the Mains.'

'They're mostly spoken for,' Cathy told him ungraciously, 'but you could have a word with my father, I suppose. He'll be in Selkirk all afternoon, but he'll be around the farm tomorrow all day.'

Amy came through from the scullery to stand beside them, watching solemnly as Cathy dried the final cup. Then, surprisingly, she put a small hand in Cathy's, drawing her towards the scullery door.

'Would you like to see my puppy?' she asked.

Margot drew in a deep breath. Perhaps they were going to be friends, after all. Cathy, with her love for animals and her high spirits, was what Amy really needed, and Ottershaws would then work the miracle she fondly hoped for.

The tension eased a little as Cathy led the way back to the scullery, but Elliott had yet to explain why the selected pup couldn't be taken from its mother immediately. Amy looked crestfallen.

'My mummy went away,' she volunteered forlornly.

Margot picked her up, holding her close.

'It will only be for a day or two,' she explained. 'Mr Dundass has promised to let you have the puppy next week, which means we must have a basket ready for her and buy a lead so that we can take her for walks.'

'We could bring her back to see Nellie,' Amy suggested, brightening perceptibly. 'It isn't very far.'

Margot looked at Elliott, but he was already making for the door where the golden Labrador, Telfer, stood wagging his tail.

'I'll deliver the pup next week,' he promised.

Cathy stood the tray upright on the scullery bench.

'I could do that,' she offered. 'I'll be taking up a pony to see how Amy manages on it, and it will save you the trouble, Elliott.'

'Perhaps you will both come,' Margot suggested impulsively. 'My father will be glad of the company.'

'Elliott may be going to London,' Cathy informed her. 'He has—something important to do there.'

She glanced at Elliott as they emerged into the sunshine, willing him to remember the promise he had made, a promise given in anger and bitterness, perhaps, but binding for all that, and Margot did not press the invitation because she was suddenly aware that Cathy was half in love with Elliott Dundass, although she was still far from understanding her own feelings of frustration and desire. They had been childhood companions, bound together by their affection for his younger brother, and now that Neil was forever lost to her Cathy was turning to Elliott on the rebound for more than sympathy and advice. Her proprietorial air was perhaps understandable in the circumstances, but Margot imagined that Elliott was much too thoughtful and introspective for this wilful girl she had hoped to befriend.

It was over a week before she saw either of them again. She had taken the car into Galashiels to do some necessary shopping when Cathy called at Ottershaws with a small brown pony to give Amy her first riding lesson, and when she returned Cathy and the pony had gone.

'You missed all the excitement,' her father told her. 'Amy was beside herself with joy.'

'And what about Cathy?' Margot asked. 'Did she agree to come again?'

'She was a bit prickly at first,' her father conceded, 'but I guess she'll mellow eventually. Basically, she's quite a nice little thing, although I think she's been spoilt lately by elderly parents. She's keen on Elliott, by the way—thinks he needs her one way or another.'

'They share a common grief,' Margot said huskily. 'It has drawn them close.'

Elliott came up the drive late the following afternoon, delivering the trembling pup in an old basket Margot had noticed at Sun Hill.

'I heard you had a new one all prepared,' he said, 'so I thought this would do in transit. The only thing left to do now is to settle on a name,' he told an ecstatic Amy, who could hardly breathe for joy.

'Will you stay for a meal?' Margot asked, when some of the excitement had died down.

He hesitated, still standing on the paved terrace outside the back door.

'I didn't intend ever to come back here like this,' he said almost brusquely. 'Ottershaws holds too many memories for me—things that are best forgotten, I suppose.'

She looked beyond him to the wide sweep of lawn where he must have played with his brother as a child.

'Wouldn't coming more often help to efface them if they are hurtful memories?' she asked. 'I've tried to make this a happy place for my family, although I have painful memories of my own.'

He turned away.

'It's your home now,' he said, 'and I think I envy

you.'

'Then stay,' she said. 'We would all like you to stay.'

While she helped Mrs Daley to prepare their evening meal, the sound of voices drifted in to them through the open window, where her father and Elliott were discussing the improvements she wanted to make in the garden, the planting of new shrubs and trees where they were needed to replenish the wood and repairs to the old tennis court which was almost obliterated by weeds. It was an environment she had often pictured in her mind's eye, and now it was here on her doorstep for her to appreciate to the full.

'You'll be wanting a hollandaise sauce with the salmon,' Elspeth Daley suggested. 'Mr Dundass is very fond of it.'

'Then we must have it,' Margot agreed, foolishly happy because Elliott Dundass was to share a meal with them in his former home.

'I'll have to give all my attention to it,' Elspeth warned. 'It's not an easy thing to make. One false step and it's curdled!'

'You concentrate and I'll do the rest,' Margot promised.

It was a simple meal, served in the panelled dining-room because they had a guest, although Margot could not think of Elliott as a guest at Ottershaws. The old house still remained his home as far as she was concerned, but he gave her no insight into his innermost thoughts as they sat talking easily enough in the gathering dusk. Amy had gone to bed late, with the pup settled in the new basket outside her bedroom door 'in case it cried for its mother in the night', and she was already asleep before Margot had looked in on her on her way down to the dining-room.

'You'll take a brandy?' her father suggested as they eventually rose from the table. 'It's early yet.'

Elliott glanced at his watch.

'It's after ten o'clock. I had no idea time would pass so quickly,' he admitted, watching as Margot prepared their coffee. 'This is all very civilised, I must admit.'

'You'll come again?' her father asked. 'Margot will be short of friends up here, just at first.'

Margot could feel Elliott's eyes on her, appraising her efforts to make a home for her family at Ottershaws.

'She has a whole long summer before her,' he answered dispassionately. 'People here are friendly enough once they get to know you. It may take a week or so to weigh you up, but once they've approved they'll go out of their way to be kind.'

'And—supposing they don't approve?' Margot asked, passing his cup.

Their eyes met, holding for a moment before he said, 'I don't think that will happen. Don't worry too much about their curiosity,' he added, perhaps thinking of Cathy or Mrs MacPhie at the post office. 'It's natural in a small community like this, especially where Ottershaws is concerned.'

'I thought they might see us as intruders,' she suggested.

He hesitated.

'I'll do my best to dispel the idea,' he promised. 'Give us time!'

Happily they discussed fishing and the countryside and all she had yet to learn about the Borders.

'I mean to buy some more books,' she told him, 'although you have plenty in the library here.'

'She's fascinated by Mary, Queen of Scots,' her father put in. 'She thinks Mary should never have married Darnley in the first place.'

'Because Bothwell was more her cup of tea,' Elliott suggested. 'He was certainly a man.'

'And a Border Reiver to boot!' Margot laughed. 'Imagine Mary riding all the way from Edinburgh to meet him in his Border tower. It defies belief!'

'She must have been in love with him,' her father suggested evenly.

'He kidnapped her!' Margot protested. 'Surely that wasn't a very sensible thing to do in the circumstances?'

'Things were different in those days,' Elliott suggested, 'and passions ran high. These hills were wild and dangerous, the border between warring kingdoms with very little respect for law and order. If you decide to spend the winter here you'll realise what I mean,' he added. 'Nature gives no quarter, and I think that's what breeds a race of determined men.'

'Without pity?' she asked.

'Not entirely.' He passed his cup to be refilled. 'Maybe we believe more in justice—paying our dues when it comes to a showdown.'

'Does it matter in the end?' Margot asked, aware of his troubled thoughts about his brother's betrayal. 'It's rather like a vendetta, isn't it?'

'Not quite the same,' he decided. 'It could be called an indulgence, I suppose—a sort of blood-letting.'

'Not just vindictive?'

'I don't think so.' He was frowning now, suddenly unsure. 'It's got to do with loyalty and so many other things.'

'The Queen married her Border Reiver in the end,' her father reflected. 'She must have been fairly sure of what she wanted.'

'I can't read about her tumultuous life without feeling a lump in my throat,' Margot confessed. 'She did her best and it all went wrong for her in the end, didn't it?'

'She lost her kingdom and her life,' Elliott agreed, 'but I think her long captivity in draughty, dank old English castles must have been the worst thing for her to bear.'

'When she was here, in her Border kingdom, she must have felt as free as a bird,' Margot mused. 'I can almost see her riding with her escort among these hills.'

'Enough of Mary!' her father decided. 'What are we going to do about this garden? Elliott has given us a free hand to plant what we like, and the tennis court will certainly prove useful once we've got it into shape again.'

'You'll come and play, if you have the time?' Margot suggested. 'My father plays well and I'm passable, and I'm sure Cathy will enjoy a game occasionally.'

'She played here quite a lot when the courts were regularly maintained,' Elliott agreed, 'and I'm sure she'll appreciate the invitation once she's thought about it. At the moment everything is horses as far as she's concerned. Did you ride out with her yesterday?'

Margot shook her head.

'I was shopping in Galashiels, but Amy was delighted. She took to her first riding lesson like a duck to water and demanded her own pony on the spot, but I think she should be content with Brown Bess for a while under Cathy's instruction.' She hesitated. 'I'd like Cathy to come here more often,' she added almost wistfully. 'They are so right together.'

'Let her take her time,' Elliott advised. 'Cathy is a mass of conflicting emotions at present, but new interests will soon colour her horizon. Anything to do with horses will be a good start,' he added with the understanding smile she had come to appreciate. 'If she doesn't respond to your invitation immediately, though, you can forget about it. She's like quicksilver.'

How well he knew this companion of his youth, Margot thought, and how tenderly he considered her, probably realising that Cathy would find it too painful to visit Ottershaws frequently as a guest because of the memories it held for her.

As for his own memories, he had locked them away for the present until he could find time to visit London, and when he left it just before midnight it was with the promise to contact her father for a day's fishing as soon as he could.

Margot walked with him to the door, opening it to a night full of stars. The whole firmament was alive with them because there had been a late frost, and there was no sound anywhere, not even the distant bleating of sheep, which she had come to associate with the hills. Even though there was no moon, they could see quite a distance to where the foothills slid down into the quiet dale where the river slid past darkly under its sheltering canopy of trees.

'It's like a painted picture,' she said quietly. 'No wonder you love it.'

'It's all I need.' He turned to look at her, his eyes dark in the starlight. 'All I need for the present,' he added. 'If it brings you the contentment you're looking for, that will be good, too. I felt uncomfortable at first, letting a stranger come here, but I don't feel like that any more. You and your father—and Amy—are right for Ottershaws, and I hope you will stay.'

She held out her hand to him.

'That's the nicest thing I've ever heard,' she confessed warmly. 'Thank you, Elliott.'

He held her hand for a brief moment of contact

which filled her with a sudden joy.

'Goodnight,' he said, 'and thank you, Margot, for a delightful meal.'

Two days later he returned with some extra equipment for her father, who had spent the previous afternoon in Galashiels buying a fishing-rod, and most of the morning was spent discussing suitable flies.

'I thought you had a flock of sheep to look after!' Margot laughed. 'Or is fly-fishing more attractive?'

'I've given myself a holiday,' he explained. 'I'm off to London as the end of the week, so I thought I'd better keep my promise about the fishing.'

'You wouldn't consider coming with us?' her father asked, gathering his gear together.

'I'd only spoil your fun,' she told him. 'Besides, there's Amy. Cathy's coming to collect her for her second riding lesson at two o'clock, but I'll cook your catch for you when you get back. I'll even put several of them in the deep-freezer,' she added wickedly, 'for future reference!'

'They don't just jump out of the water into the landing-net,' her father admonished, 'and I'll have to get my hand in again.'

Elliott slung his bag over his shoulder.

'I'll promise you at least one fish,' he said.

When Cathy had collected Amy and they had ridden away together along the moor track, Margot spent a useful afternoon in the garden thinking about the two men down by the river and the easy companionship which seemed to be developing between them. Was this what she really wanted, she wondered, to be here for the rest of her life, living it out in a quiet place away from the turmoil and stress of a successful career driving her ever onwards? The competition was always hard at first, the striving and the ever-present desire to do better, but she supposed she had been born to sing. If she had to give it up——

She paused before the alarming thought, unable to come to any decision, although during her sojourn here in this clear, clean atmosphere her voice had become stronger. Some of the huskiness had already gone, and she had caught herself singing in the morning before her open window for sheer joy only the day before.

It was a sign that she should go back to London, she supposed, for that final check-up and a chance to consider her long-term future, but she had also to think of Amy. There was no way that she could turn her over completely to yet another housekeeper or even a nanny.

It was a decision for the future, she told herself—perhaps the distant future.

Restlessly she waited till the two men returned, walking to the moor gate to meet them as the westering sun went behind a passing cloud, casting its dark shadow on the hills. Their combined effort on the river had produced only one fish.

'It'll never do for five of us,' she pointed out, seeing Cathy and her pupil approaching from the moor. 'I can't work miracles!'

'I'll relieve you of the necessity,' Elliott smiled. 'I must get back to Sun Hill.'

Yet he lingered at the gate as Cathy and Amy rode through into the garden to follow her father to the house.

'Will you be in London for any length of time?' she asked.

'For no more than a day or two, I hope.' His whole expression changed as he looked beyond her to the shadow on the hills. 'I have something to do there—something important. I have to find someone to tell her what I think of her. I have to get it out of my system before I can settle into my life at Sun Hill.'

Disconcerted, Margot looked back into his angry eyes.

'It must be important to you,' she said huskily. 'Is there no other way?'

'None,' he decided. 'My brother went to London two years ago when he should have stayed at Ottershaws where he belonged. He had some sort of idea that he could make it big there.'

'What did he want to do?' Margot asked, sensing his bitter disillusionment. She could see that the subject was painful to him, but she persisted because she thought it might help if he was able to talk about it to someone with an open mind and not just Cathy. 'It must have been quite different from sheep-farming.'

'He thought he could write and he had done some local articles and helped to put on a play at the Edinburgh Festival, but apparently London was a different kettle of fish and he sensed the competition as soon as he got there. We didn't hear from him for over a year after that. It was as if he had just disappeared into thin air and there was very little we could do about it.'

She put a sympathetic hand on his arm.

'London's like that,' she admitted. 'It swallows you up. You are so busy making a career that you forget how quickly time flies when you are meeting new people and absorbing so many new ideas. Don't blame Neil too much. You see,' she added slowly, 'I know quite a lot about it. I had a promising career there before I felt that I had to come away for a while, but my agent is still pressing me to return. He thinks I owe it to myself—and possibly to him—to go back as quickly as I can.'

He regarded her stonily for a moment.

'Were you an actress?' he asked.

'No. I was a singer. Not right out there in front, you understand, but reasonably successful,' she admitted. 'I was in demand and my agent assures me I am only at the beginning of things.'

He looked down at her, a dark fire in his eyes.

'And will you change your mind and go back?' he demanded.

'I don't know. These past few weeks I've found it hard to make up my mind about my long-term future, even with the thought of Amy settled here and my father content.'

Sudden accusation supplanted the fire in his eyes.

'Do you mean to leave Amy here alone?' he asked coldly.

'She would have my father to look after her.'

'And some other woman? That wouldn't be the same,' he declared. 'How could it be? She needs the love and protection of her own family so that she can give them love in return. She is your child. You ought to look after her.'

Margot took a time to answer him, realising the mistake he had made.

'You're wrong, Elliott,' she said. 'Amy is my niece—my brother's child, but I must tell you about that some time and perhaps you will understand how I feel. I am hesitating now because I do love Amy and I want her to grow up a healthy, normal little girl with no inhibitions to cloud her horizons. Surely you don't blame me for that?'

He drew a deep breath.

'Perhaps I blame you for wanting to return to London so soon,' he said, 'but that might be completely natural when it seems to hold so much for you in the future.'

Was he asking her to stay for more than Amy's sake? Her heart bounded with urgent joy, but when she looked into his eyes there was nothing there but the

return of his former resolve. Remembering the scene in
the hotel lounge, she could hear the cry of anguish in
Cathy's voice as she denounced his brother's unfaithful
lover: 'You must go in search of her, Elliott. You must
punish her for what she has done.'

'I wish I could help you,' she said unhappily.

'No one can do that.' The old hardness steeled his
jaw. 'This is something I have to do for myself.'

'And Cathy?' she asked.

His gaze went beyond her to the shadowed hills.

'Perhaps for Cathy, too,' he agreed. 'She loved Neil.
All their lives they were together till he went to London.
He promised to write to her, but he never did, and now
he is dead because of someone he met there. We'll
never forgive her for what she did—never!'

'How are you going to find her—this woman you
hate so much?' she found herself asking.

'I'm not sure about that, but I'll go on searching for
her whenever I can. It may not do any good to let her
know what I think of her, because I have a feeling she is
the selfish kind who will never give Neil a thought now
that he is dead. It would appear that her career meant
more than anything else to her, her journey to the top
and her ruthless ambition to get there as quickly as she
could.'

'Have you any idea who she was—any way of finding
out?' she asked.

'I have a diary of Neil's sent here among his personal
effects.' He was finding it difficult to speak of these
things, she realised. 'Her name is Olivia Hallam and
I've got to find her.' He turned to face her. 'You do
realise that, don't you?'

Stricken, she gazed back at him as if she could not
understand what he had just told her.

'Olivia Hallam,' she repeated through frozen lips.
'Elliott, you must be mistaken——'

'I'm not mistaken,' he said, turning away. 'I know

that I have to find her now that I have discovered her name and who she is.'

Oh, not who she is! She watched him go in silence, her own name echoing like thunder in her ears. Her professional name!

CHAPTER THREE

BEING Olivia Hallam had been so utterly fulfilling in the past. It had been her mother's name, and she had adopted it when Henry Levitt had considered Margot Kennedy not quite professional enough, but now it sounded like a knell in her ears. The death knell of love. How could she ever tell Elliott that she was the woman he sought, the woman responsible for his brother's disillusionment, if not his ultimate downfall? How could she confess to being Olivia Hallam, when her feelings for him and her growing love for him had become the dominant part of her life at Ottershaws?

Yet, when she thought about it more calmly, she could not remember anyone called Neil Dundass, a name she would have recognised long ago.

Her impulse was to confess all even before Elliott left for London in search of her, but she knew that if she did he might hate her forever. So, with confusion clouding her judgement and the dawning love in her heart, she did nothing.

When the letter from Harley Street arrived two days later, confirming her appointment with the specialist, she made her plans to travel south, leaving Mrs Daley in command at Ottershaws.

'I'll only be away for one night,' she told Amy. 'I'll soon be back home.'

Her father drove her to Berwick-on-Tweed to join the Edinburgh to London Inter-City train.

'No need to drive all that way,' he had advised. 'I'll be at the station to meet you when you get back. Just phone.'

'I may be away for more than one day,' she said.
'I'll have to see Henry when I've heard the
specialist's verdict.'

'I think it might be good news,' he predicted,
standing on the high, windy platform waiting for the
train to draw out. 'You're looking well, and your
voice isn't half so husky as it was three weeks ago.
Border air must be working a miracle!'

Could it be only three weeks since she had first
crossed the Border? Margot wondered as the train
drew away from the platform. Looking down at the
broad, clear Tweed flowing beneath her as the train
crossed the bridge, she could hardly believe how
quickly the time had passed. 'When you are happy,'
her mother used to say, 'time goes far too quickly.'
And the last few years had certainly proved her right.
Her student days at the Royal Academy had been the
happiest days of her life so far, when nothing but
music had mattered to her, and her full mezzo-
soprano voice had marked her down for success. She
had sung in *Carmen* at the Coliseum and in
Tchaikovsky's *Eugene Onegin* at Covent Garden, and
it was there that she had met Henry Levitt, who had
become her agent and also her friend.

When she thought of Henry a new warmth stole
over her. He had taken her by the hand to lead her
forward, giving her the confidence she needed. His
confidence in her future had never faltered for one
second, and he had given her the assurance she
needed to get up on that stage and sing.

Long before she reached London she was beginning to feel guilty about Henry. He had done so much
for her and she knew how disappointed he had been
when her voice had failed. They had shared so much,
and it hadn't seemed to matter that Henry was older
and much, much wiser than she was. She had taken
his advice unquestioningly in the past, assured that

her professional welfare and her ultimate happiness
were first priorities as far as he was concerned, but she
also knew that he had given her his friendship, which
meant a great deal to her. Henry was no more a
Svengali than her father had been; they had both
believed in her talent and wanted her to succeed.

Her four o'clock appointment in Harley Street gave
her time for a meal, after which she phoned Henry's
office.

'In London?' he said, surprised when he heard her
voice. 'But why didn't you let me know you were
coming? I could have met your train.'

'I wanted to see Mr Carlton first,' she explained, 'and
I needed time to think. Can we meet this evening?'

'Any time,' he assured her. 'We'll find somewhere
quiet where we can have a meal and talk.'

'I'm staying at the Kendal,' she explained.

'OK. I'll pick you up there at seven. Meanwhile we'll
keep our fingers crossed, because I've got some good
news for you!'

'Good news?' she repeated. 'What about?' She was
immediately alert. 'Henry, I can't promise you anything
till I've seen Mr Carlton at four o'clock.'

'I've an idea what the verdict might be,' he assured
her in his breezy way. 'I haven't heard a sound of
hoarseness in your voice since I lifted the receiver and
realised it was you.'

'We mustn't cross our bridges before we come to
them,' she warned.

'I think we've come to this one,' he said with
assurance. 'You sound as if the Scottish air has done
you a power of good. Anyway, we'll talk about that
when we meet. Keep your chin up and think of
America!'

Before the virus had struck he had been negotiating a
flight for her to New York to audition for a famous
music director, and now it seemed she was about to be

given another chance. Six years of hard work and dedication were finally paying off for her, and she ought to be grateful when, at twenty-four, a brilliant career could lie ahead of her; so why was it that her enthusiasm wasn't soaring to the clouds? Doubt and indecision should have no place in her calculations, although it might be some time yet before her voice was back to full strength and power, but curiously the doubt remained.

When she had washed and changed, she walked the short distance to Harley Street, standing for a moment at the massive, black-painted door before she finally rang the bell. This was it! This was the way ahead, or the journey back to another career.

A tall, middle-aged secretary showed her into the waiting-room on the ground floor.

'Mr Carlton will see you in a moment,' she said kindly. 'He's speaking on the telephone.'

Margot cleared her throat.

'Thank you,' she said.

Of course she was nervous, she told herself. It was only natural when so much depended upon the verdict she was about to hear. She sat with her hands clasped tightly before her, wondering about the future until the door opened and Andrew Carlton looked in at her.

'You've brought some good weather with you,' he observed. 'What was it like in Scotland?'

'Beautiful!' Her voice was husky again. 'I—really didn't want to leave.'

'I know what you mean,' he said. 'I trained in Edinburgh and I thought I'd never settle down here at first, but now I'm getting used to it, although I'm off to the west of Scotland whenever I get the chance. I was born there,' he explained, holding open the door for her.

It took him less than ten minutes to give her his verdict.

'Everything is satisfactory so far,' he said. 'Another six months should see you back to normal.'

'Six months?' Margot echoed, dismayed.

'Don't be too disappointed,' he said. 'We mustn't rush things. I want to be quite sure, you see, that no damage whatever has been done, and that will take time. And patience on your part, I'm afraid,' he added. 'I don't want you to strain your vocal cords at all. No singing, not even a practice. The time will soon pass.'

She went out into the sunshine feeling that she had been given some sort of reprieve, when really she should have been disappointed. What's the matter with me, she thought, and what can I possibly say to Henry?

Walking back along Wigmore Street in the sunshine, she could only think of Ottershaws and the sanctuary it offered her for another six months.

Henry picked her up at seven o'clock as he had promised. He was a dapper little man in his early forties with a round, open face and dark brown eyes under beetling eyebrows which rose expressively as he greeted her with a kiss on each cheek.

'What news?' he asked, leading her down the steps to the taxi waiting for them at the kerb. 'You look radiant.'

Margot hesitated.

'It isn't good news, Henry, as far as my career is concerned,' she told him. 'I've another six months to wait.'

'How come?' he asked. 'You sound a hundred per cent to me.'

'There's just a risk,' she explained. 'We've got to give it time. If I sing again too soon, apparently it could cause irreparable damage to my vocal cords. I can't even practise.'

He waited until they were in the taxi before he said,

'This is terrible. I was going to tell you that you had everything going for you. The audition in New York is on again, and I was sure you would be able to make it this time, since it's important.'

She sensed his frustration and some underlying anger.

'Henry, I'm sorry!' She put her hand over his. 'I expected to have better news for you, but——'

'But?' he prompted.

'I really couldn't have come back to London so soon.'

'How do you make that out?' he demanded.

Margot hesitated for the second time.

'You know I have Amy to consider,' she said.

Henry, who had no great reserve of patience, immediately blew his top.

'Amy?' he repeated. 'You may have Amy but you don't have time! It's now or never, Margot. Making a comeback after a year or so won't be easy. You ought to know that. This offer from New York will establish you worldwide, and that was what you wanted most, wasn't it?'

She looked out of the taxi window at the crowded London streets. Before Ottershaws, she thought, but she only had Ottershaws for a little while—less than three short years before the lease would finally run out—and in that time Elliott could marry and want to move back into his old home to raise a family where, in his youth, he had known so much happiness for so long.

'I know the odds,' she acknowledged, 'but I can't do anything about it for the present. I can't fly in the face of the specialist's opinion. Surely you realise that?'

'Yes,' he said. 'I'm sorry—sorry and disappointed and damnably frustrated, because I wanted this for you more than anyone. I believed in you.'

'Oh, Henry,' she said, 'I know how hard you have tried.'

'It's my job,' he acknowledged despondently. 'I do my best.'

'Yes, I know. Forgive me!'

He heaved a sigh.

'I had such plans for you,' he confessed. Then, brightening, 'Something else will turn up when you're ready. We'll not talk about it any more just now.'

'You understand me so well!'

'I think you are far too conscientious about that family of yours,' he growled. 'Now that you have them firmly established in Scotland, I can't see that you have to do anything more. The child isn't your responsibility.'

'I have to take care of Amy till her father comes back,' Margot said firmly.

'And when will that be?' he enquired drily.

'I don't know. He keeps in touch, of course, but he's been abroad now for three years. He never got over his wife's death, you see. Emily died in childbirth and he always refused to acknowledge Amy, although he was willing to pay for her upkeep and a suitable nurse. I suppose he blamed her for her mother's death in a way —taking Emily from him at the beginning of their marriage. It wasn't fair, of course, but these things never are on the tiny victim. Every time I write to him I ask him to at least pay us a visit to see Amy as she is now, in the hope that it will bring them together. Amy is so like her mother that some of his desperate love must rub off on her child.'

'It could have the opposite effect,' he warned.

'I'm hoping not, because I hope he will come quite soon,' Margot said. 'I know he has leave to take, and he won't want to spend it in Bahrain.'

During their lunch they tried to speak of other things, about the world of music to which they both belonged and about Ottershaws which Margot tried to describe to him.

'You must come and see for yourself,' she urged as

they rose to leave the restaurant.

'And what would I do in Scotland where there's nothing but heather and mist?' he demanded.

'That's not true, and you know it!' she returned. 'At least you could come for the Edinburgh Festival.'

'Which is months away,' he reminded her. 'I hope to see you back in London before then and ready to go to New York. I can't save this audition, but there will be others.' He looked at her keenly as they moved towards the revolving doors. 'You may be gentle and softly spoken, Margot, but I know about all the fires that are burning under that calm face you present to the public.'

'Now you are just being provocative!' she laughed, adding more soberly, 'I do care about my career, Henry, but—sometimes I wonder if there isn't something more, something even more fulfilling than success, down another road.'

'Don't think about it,' he said, hailing a taxi. 'There's nothing more fulfilling than a successful career. I can guarantee you that much.'

With doubt in her heart, she let him drop her at her hotel. It was a doubt which baffled her in a good many ways, and one she would have to come to terms with in the near future, she supposed, but there was also the thought of her return to Ottershaws to chase it away.

She did some necessary shopping and took a taxi to King's Cross the following morning, still unconvinced that she would be back in the metropolis in six months' time with Henry still willing to pull out all the stops in her musical career.

Travelling on a Friday was anything but wise, she discovered as she joined the substantial queue waiting at the barrier, but she had a seat booked for her return journey and there was really no need to contemplate standing all the way to Berwick. Ahead of her in the crowd she imagined that she caught a glimpse of Elliott Dundass, but that was purely supposition conjured up, perhaps, by the thought of him. It was too much of a coincidence, yet he had been in London for almost a week.

When she finally reached the ticket barrier, the tall, distinguished-looking man who had stood head and shoulders above his fellow travellers had disappeared. He had gone on ahead to find his carriage, and she must look for her own seat, yet as she walked along the platform she was aware of searching for Elliott Dundass in that unlikely place, and her heart began to pound as she scanned her fellow passengers who had already taken their seats. He was nowhere to be seen.

She found her reservation and put her coat and overnight bag on the rack above her. Presently she would go along the corridor for lunch.

Opening the newspaper she had bought, she scanned the headlines, but they were much as she had expected: an abortive hijack here and a political scandal there—nothing new. Laying the paper aside, she gazed at the passing scene, green fields and a blue April sky under which tiny English villages, steeped in peace, lay comfortably in the sun. No hills, nothing remotely dramatic in that gentle landscape—not even sheep!

She was thinking about Ottershaws again, and the rolling, shadow-haunted hills which she was beginning to accept as home.

Booked for the second sitting at lunch, she went along to the restaurant-car when it was finally announced, and when the automatic door slid open at her tread she saw Elliott standing at a table for two. He had a folded newspaper under his arm which he tossed into the overhead rack before he sat down.

She drew a deep breath of relief, although somewhere inside she was also aware of a note of panic.

'Can I sit beside you?' she asked as he looked up and recognised her. 'I thought I saw you going through the ticket barrier at King's Cross, although I wasn't sure.'

He got to his feet.

'Of course,' he said, the frown disappearing from his brow. 'What are you doing here?'

'I've been in London, seeing my agent,' she explained.

'And?' he asked briefly.

'Oh—it was only a routine trip. I'm not going back.' She settled into the seat facing him. 'I also had a check-up in Harley Street.' Her voice was husky again. 'I haven't had a definite all clear.'

'And that was a disappointment?' he suggested.

'I suppose it was,' she admitted. 'I wanted to be told I was a hundred per cent, but I'm not supposed to sing for another six months, at least.'

'I'm sorry,' he said conventionally.

'I have to accept it.' She studied the menu, aware of a nervousness she could not quite control. 'You didn't stay very long in the big city.'

'No.' The wine steward came to stand beside them. 'What will you drink?'

'I need something long and cool,' she decided. 'Cinzano and lemonade will do.'

They sat in silence for a moment, looking pleased to see each other, although there was a question hovering at the back of her mind. Had his quest been successful? Had he discovered what he wanted to know about Olivia Hallam? She dared not look into his eyes again in case she would find her answer there, but how could he possibly denounce her in their present circumstances? He would keep his rigid cool until some other occasion presented itself.

When their soup was served she tried to say lightly, 'There's an art in this sort of thing. You wait till the train has finished jolting and then you cope as best you can!'

He looked across the table at her without anger.

'I always hope it doesn't land in my lap,' he agreed. 'How was Ottershaws looking when you left?'

It seemed that he had always Ottershaws in mind because it was closest to his heart.

'Ablaze with daffodils,' she told him. 'I must confess I didn't want to come away.'

Which was true enough, she thought, feeling that they both agreed about this, at least.

'And Amy?' he enquired.

'Oh—she and Cathy are hand-in-glove now. They can think of nothing but dogs and ponies. It's such a wonderful thing for Amy because she has missed so much. Her mother died soon after she was born, and my brother has been abroad ever since, working in Bahrain.'

'Surely he has leave?' he suggested.

'Yes, but he prefers to take it elsewhere, I'm afraid. One day, though, I hope he will come to Scotland to be with us for a while,' she added.

'And that will make a difference to your career?'

He was watching her closely, a definite question in his eyes.

'It would give me more freedom—yes,' she admitted, 'but I wonder if that is what I really want. It's all quite difficult, Elliott, being torn between two desires—two loves, if you like. All my life so far I've thought in terms of a career, and for six years I've studied with that in mind, but now——'

She looked out at the hurrying scene, aware that he was waiting for her immediate conclusion.

'I'd like to think I'd got my voice back one hundred per cent,' she added. 'Of course I would, but I don't know about going to New York. It's the ultimate destination—the Metropolitan Opera—but it's something you have to think very carefully about. It's a hard slog, and other things would have to be put aside.'

'Such as?'

'Home-life, for one,' she found herself confessing. 'The chance to enjoy somewhere like Ottershaws for a while, at least.'

'Is that important to you?' He asked the question directly, looking into her shadowed eyes.

'It has become important,' she answered slowly. 'More important than I ever thought possible. It's really difficult for me to explain.'

'Not to me,' he returned, 'and not just because of Ottershaws. We seem to share the same deep desire for roots somewhere in the past.'

'You have all the roots you need at Ottershaws and Sun Hill,' she reminded him.

'And somehow it is not enough. I went to London hoping to clear something out of my mind,' he added deliberately, 'and I haven't been successful.'

Her heart seemed to miss a beat, wondering what he was about to say, but she couldn't bring herself to ask about Olivia Hallam. Something in her recoiled at the thought of what he might tell her, some stricken, helpless thing quivering in her heart.

'I'm sorry!' She looked down at her clenched hands. 'I thought you might have—cleared everything up.'

'I learned very little.' His mouth clamped into a hard line. 'I still have only Neil's diaries to go on, and I still haven't had time to read them all. When I got to the flat, the person he had shared it with had gone. He didn't seem to be a very stable character anyway, so I don't suppose he could have told me very much. I collected what was left of Neil's belongings and came away.'

'Was there—nobody else?' she asked huskily.

'Nobody who could have helped. People seem to vanish into thin air in London if they want to move on without leaving any trace behind them, but I don't mean to give up,' he added sternly. 'I'll find Olivia Hallam sooner or later, if it takes me a lifetime.'

'Elliott——' She was still looking down at her clenched hands, knowing that she should tell him the

truth now and not at some future date when he would
hate her more than ever for her deception, but her
growing feelings for him were at war with her impulse
to confess all, because she had accepted the sure
knowledge that he would never forgive her for what he
believed she had done. To tell him the truth now would
undermine the love he had for the brother who had
shared his life for so long.

'What were you going to say?' he asked.

'I—nothing. Tell me what you did with the rest of
your stay in London,' she suggested.

'Not very much. By the time I had seen my brother's
solicitor and cleared up his affairs, it was time to come
home. I don't regret that,' he added, 'although I will
have to go back. I have more information to go on
now— more evidence.' Suddenly he was avoiding the
issue as she had done. 'I've been thinking about
Ottershaws a lot—what you are trying to do there—and
I appreciate it, but some things remain my responsibility. Such as the tennis court,' he added. 'I mean to
pay my share.'

'That isn't necessary,' she returned quickly,
conscious of a vast relief now that they were treading
safer ground. 'We'll be the ones who are using it.'

'And Cathy—and me occasionally,' he pointed out,
the darkness gone from his face. 'I can't allow you to
make all the improvements on your own.'

'Because you might feel you are in my debt?' she
suggested, well aware of his native pride.

'Not entirely.' He looked deeply into her eyes,
smiling faintly. 'Not just that. You can call it a sense of
fairness, if you like. The property is mine and you are
improving it out of all proportion. I want to do my
share.'

'A joint project,' she said. 'Perhaps I shouldn't argue
against that.'

'I hope you won't. You've done so much for

Ottershaws as it is, turning it into a home again.'

She considered the word wistfully as the steward changed their plates.

'It wasn't very hard to do,' she said. 'The basic ingredients were already there.'

When they spoke about Ottershaws, everything else slid into the background and soon they were discussing the planting of more trees and necessary repairs to the old coach-house which was now used as a garage.

'In a place like Ottershaws you can conjure up the past so clearly,' she mused. 'Horses and a carriage and no great desire to rush away, except perhaps to Edinburgh for a concert in the winter or a shopping spree!'

'My mother certainly thought like that,' he admitted, taking her quite easily into his confidence. 'She was really a Victorian at heart, although she also kept in touch with the current scene. There were great parties at Ottershaws in those days, cousins and friends always there, and we bred horses. It was something we had in common with the Graemes,' he added, bringing Cathy's name into the conversation quite naturally. 'We lived in each other's pockets, I suppose, but Border families are like that. We must take you to the Riding of the Marches and introduce you to tradition,' he suggested unexpectedly.

'I'd like that,' she agreed spontaneously. 'When is it done?'

'Oh, not till the autumn,' he told her, giving some of his attention to the main course he had ordered. 'There's plenty of time for that.'

And time for you to find out all about Olivia Hallam, she thought, her heart contracting with sudden pain. Time for all this to slip away from me forever.

'Are you being met at Berwick?' he asked. 'If not, I can give you a lift. I came over in the Range Rover and left it there.'

She had to refuse his offer.

'My father will be at Berwick with the car,' she explained. 'If we had known——'

'I should have thought of that,' he said, 'but perhaps another time? I'd like you to see the Borders as they really are.'

With you, she thought, realising that she would see so much more through his eyes, all the beauty and all the drama of that lovely land.

They sat in the restaurant-car over their coffee until they were well into Northumberland, where the beautiful indented coastline revealed breathtaking views of the blue North Sea.

'It's not always like this,' he told her. 'It can live up to its reputation of the "dark North Sea" quite easily, but when the sun shines it's transformed.'

Beauty turned into terror, she thought. Thor 'striking on his anvil in his smithy by the dark North Sea'!

'Do beauty and happiness never last?' she asked, as a chilling shiver ran over her, reminding her of the confession she had still to make.

'I don't know. We take them very much for granted, but perhaps we make or mar our own happiness.'

'I don't want to do that,' she admitted, 'but——'

He looked across the table at her as she hesitated.

'I can't imagine you making a mistake,' he said.

'I've made so many,' she confessed. 'I've been swayed so often by indecision and regret.'

'But you have also been successful, I gather. You surely can't have any regrets about your career?'

'That wasn't quite what I meant.' Should she tell him who she was now, or wait for a more convenient time? 'My career has been successful up to a point, but now it could go either way. What I'm trying to face is the fact that it doesn't seem to be all that important at the moment. I have to learn to wait.'

He rose to return to his own carriage, helping her into

her jacket, his hand brushing momentarily against her cheek to send the blood pulsing through her veins as if he had kissed her.

'Thank you,' she said unsteadily. 'Perhaps I'll see you at Berwick.'

She went along the swaying carriages knowing now that Elliott meant more than just a landlord to her and that she had reached some sort of crossroads in her life. One way was leading her back to success in her chosen career, the other . . .

She glanced out at the bright North Sea. Was the other way leading her to Elliott Dundass and conflict and pain? One day she would have to tell him the truth, and how could she bear to stay at Ottershaws once he knew? She thought of his lone search in London for Olivia Hallam, when all the time she had been there, almost in his arms.

CHAPTER FOUR

MARGOT'S father met the train at Berwick, obviously surprised to see them together.

'If we had known,' Elliott said, 'we could have saved you the journey.'

The two men shook hands.

'I had nothing else to do,' Andrew Kennedy returned. 'Amy is off half the day with Cathy, and Mrs Daley organises everything around the house, so I've been exploring a bit, seeing the countryside.'

'What about the fishing?' Elliott asked.

'I haven't got around to that. I plan to go tomorrow.'

Elliott hesitated.

'If you can make it the day after that, I'll take you down to a stretch of water I know very well,' he offered. 'There's a great hole there where I've always pulled in plenty of fish.'

Andrew looked pleased.

'Why don't we all go?' he suggested. 'Margot should learn to cast a fly.'

'I wouldn't have the heart to hook a fish and pull it out,' Margot said, 'but I wouldn't say no to a picnic. That way, we could all enjoy the river.'

A real family outing, she thought. A day on the river not soon to be forgotten.

'I'll provide the food,' she offered, 'and bring it down in a basket. I haven't enjoyed a picnic in years!'

Elliott smiled at her enthusiasm.

'I know exactly the spot,' he promised, moving towards the Range Rover he had parked in the station yard almost a week ago. 'I'll call for you at ten o'clock. If it is too bright a day for fishing, we can always enjoy Margot's picnic.'

Margot got into the car beside her father.

'What made you think of that?' she asked, watching as Elliott reversed the Range Rover. 'Casting flies, when you know I'll be no good at it?'

'It's called being neighbourly,' he said, letting in the clutch. 'I don't think Dundass ought to be such a recluse, and he did offer to take me,' he reminded her.

'But not the whole family!' she protested with sudden happiness welling in her heart. 'You suggested that.'

'Why not? I considered the fact that we have to eat to survive, and a picnic was the best solution. Amy will love it.'

'We do a lot for Amy,' Margot mused. 'I wish James would realise, though, that she needs him, too. We can't act as proxy father for him for ever. It's just not fair.'

'It certainly isn't fair as far as Amy is concerned,' he admitted, 'and perhaps not fair to you, either. How did the Harley Street consultation go?'

'I'm improving, but it will take at least another six months before I can sing again.'

'Do you regret the fact?' He stole a sideways glance at her flushed face. 'You seem to be content enough as you are.'

'I am, for the time being.'

'And what might that mean?'

She drew a deep breath.

'I feel that I may not be able to stay in Scotland for ever.'

'Had you thought of Ottershaws permanently?'

'Elliott wouldn't sell—not ever, but I suppose I thought I could make a base here—somewhere to come back to when I wasn't working.'

'Supposing you marry?' he suggested. 'There's

always the possibility,' he pointed out when she didn't answer immediately.

'I—don't think so.' Her voice was hoarse again. 'I've never quite found the right person up till now.'

He waited for her to continue, but she could not tell him that she had fallen in love with Eliott Dundass in so short a time.

'I can't talk about it,' she said. 'Not yet. Tell me all you've been doing while I've been away.'

'Exploring mostly. This is a lovely country, Margot. I'm just sorry I didn't discover it before.'

'Itchy feet!' She smiled. 'You were never in England for very long. Perhaps,' she suggested, 'that's why James stays away.'

'You know it isn't,' he said. 'It's because of Emily. He can't bear to look at Amy because he believes she caused her mother's death. That's the way he thinks, and perhaps we have made it too easy for him, accepting his child in the way we have for so long.'

'What else could we have done?' Margot protested. 'Even as a tiny baby she wrapped her fingers round our hearts. I've written to James so many times,' she added wistfully, 'suggesting that he should at least visit us, but you know the result. Even when we were living in London he could always find the necessary excuse.'

'Has he replied to your last letter?'

She shook her head. 'But that's quite normal,' she pointed out. 'He always seems so busy.'

'I'm prepared to believe he is,' Andrew Kennedy conceded, 'but not twenty-four hours a day. Being busy is really no excuse.'

'I sent him some photographs,' Margot said. 'I think he ought to see how Amy has grown.'

'It must have been difficult for him at first,' her father acknowledged. 'A new-born infant is such a helpless thing, and it was so near to his devastating loss, but now it is well over four years and Amy is a delight, you have to admit,' he added quietly. 'She ought to get to know her father.'

They drove in silence for the next few miles, thinking their separate thoughts.

'Do you want some tea?' Andrew asked when they reached Kelso.

'I'd rather go straight home,' Margot decided.

He glanced at her for a brief moment.

'You said that as if you had lived at Ottershaws all your life,' he commented.

Margot's smile deepened.

'It's such a different life—belonging somewhere like this where your family has lived for generations instead of moving from place to place.'

'As we have been doing,' he suggested. 'Yes, I suppose it is, but we're all made differently, Margot. Perhaps some of my own wanderlust has rubbed off on James now, so I'm particularly to blame.'

'I don't think so,' Margot said. 'Anyway, we've got the next six months to be happy in,' she added, although she was still aware of the deep sense of guilt lying against her heart when she thought about Elliott.

Elliott came to Ottershaws early, as he had promised, finding her in the kitchen cutting sandwiches.

'You look as if you're preparing for a siege,' he teased.

'I've heard how hungry fishermen can get.' She wondered if he could hear the quick drumming of her heart as he watched her. 'Have you brought the Range Rover?'

'At your service!' He sampled a sandwich.

'That's cheating!' she laughed. 'You're getting more than your share.'

When he did not answer, she turned to look at him.

'Margot,' he said, his blue, penetrating eyes peculiarly gentle now, 'I never thought I would be

able to come back here like this, to see someone else in
my mother's kitchen and so much being done around
the estate without my help. You've made a great difference to Ottershaws already, and I thank you for it.'

They were very close, close enough to hear each
other's heartbeats, Margot thought, close enough to
touch, yet he made no movement towards her, and she
could only stand there, remembering how much she
had to tell him that he surely had to know.

I'm Olivia Hallam. Her lips almost formed the fatal
words, although she could not utter them. Not yet, she
thought, not on a day like this when the sun was shining so brightly and they were going off on a picnic
together to a secret place which he had always loved.

'I'll put some lemonade in for Amy,' she said
urgently before she handed over the basket. 'She wants
us to take the pup, by the way. Do you think that might
be in order?'

'I don't see why not. He's old enough now to walk as
far as the river, if you mean to walk.'

'So long as he doesn't scare the fish!' Margot said. 'If
you take my father down in the Range Rover with all
the gear, I'll bring Amy—and the pup.'

'Have you found a name for him yet?' he asked,
strapping up the picnic basket for her. 'He'll learn to
answer to it quite quickly.'

She smoothed her hair in front of the kitchen mirror.

'You're going to laugh at this,' she warned. 'Amy
wants to call him Duster.'

He smiled at the idea.

'There must be a reason.'

'I think it's because his tail sweeps the low tables in
the drawing-room and most of the kitchen floor!'

'It makes a change from Nell and Spot,' he
acknowledged. 'Amy is quite a girl!'

Margot looked through the open door where Amy
was greeting Cathy.

'She's changed so much during the past few weeks—opened out a lot, which must be due to Cathy. They're almost inseparable now,' Margot acknowledged.

The pup was welcoming the newcomer with his usual exuberance, but Cathy's eyes were strangely hard.

'I didn't know you were going off for the day,' she said without looking directly at either of them. 'I brought the ponies over for Amy to have another lesson.'

For a moment Margot hesitated, conscious of intrusion, before she said heartily enough, 'Why don't you come with us, Cathy? We're only going down to the river to fish.'

Cathy glanced at the Range Rover and back again to the basket in Elliott's hand.

'What—all of you?' she asked.

'Oh, I'm not going to fish,' Margot said. 'I'm going to walk down later in time for lunch.'

Cathy swung round to confront Elliott at last.

'Where are you taking them?' she asked.

'To the stretch of water below the middle pool.'

'Neil's pool?' All the colour had drained out of Cathy's face. 'How could you go there,' she demanded, 'so soon?'

Elliott put the hamper into the back of the Range Rover.

'I have to go there sooner or later, Cathy,' he said. 'It's the stretch of water I know best. I've fished it with Neil—yes, but there's a lot of other things to make us remember him round here, and we can't shun them for ever. Perhaps it would be better if you came down to the pool with us,' he added quite gently. 'It might make things easier for you afterwards.'

Cathy glared at him.

'I don't know how you could do this,' she cried. 'Taking strangers there!'

'Think about it,' Elliott said, 'and come if you can.'

Amy was as eager as ever to go off with Cathy for an hour, and when they returned Cathy had obviously changed her mind about the picnic by the riverside.

'Amy and I can ride down,' she suggested, accepting the mug of coffee Margot prepared for her, 'and you can follow with Duster.'

For some reason she had decided not to let Elliott out of her sight, to be with him at his brother's favourite pool while they both faced the future without Neil.

Margot decided not to let the unexpected little incident upset her too much. This was going to be her day, the day she had thought about ever since Elliott and her father had arranged it at Berwick, and Cathy digging up the past was not going to spoil it for her. Elliott had almost suggested to Cathy that they should put the past behind them, bit by bit, and she was going to do that, too, although it would rear its head again when she finally told Elliott the truth.

It was little more than a mile to the pool. Cathy and Amy rode ahead of her, while Duster pulled strongly on his new lead, eager to get there before everyone else. He was a strong little dog with softly expressive brown eyes and a gloriously wagging tail, forever trying to cross the narrow road beside the river to see what lay on the other side.

'Sorry about the lead!' she told him happily. 'But you must bear with it till we get to the pool.'

Elliott and her father had established themselves in the shade of some trees casting a necessary shadow over the dark water below.

'Any luck?' she called to them from the road above.

'Not a sausage!' Andrew lamented. 'They must have seen me coming!'

She went over the fence and down the grassy bank towards him, seeing Elliott thigh-deep in the water only a short distance away.

'How about your companion in crime?' she asked.

Andrew shrugged.

'Nothing. The light isn't too good.'

Cathy and Amy were tethering the ponies to the fence.

'We've come for the picnic,' Amy announced.

'You'll have to wait a bit. It's only twelve o'clock,' her grandfather pointed out, wading downstream a little. 'And you mustn't shout, or it will scare the fish,' he cautioned.

Elliott reeled in his line and came towards them.

'Care to try your hand?' he asked, offering Margot a spare rod.

'I don't know the first thing about it,' she protested.

'You can try,' he encouraged her. 'There are no exams to pass.'

Landing-nets, spare rods and waterproof jackets were scattered on the grass, with a selection of flies resting in a special box near a group of stones which would be ideal for their picnic. Everything seemed perfect: the sun, the sheltering trees, the deep, cool river sliding in and out of the silent pool, and Amy standing full of curiosity on the bank with Cathy by her side.

Elliott selected a fly.

'Try this one,' he said. 'It's good for beginners!'

Margot tossed back her hair to look up at him.

'You're joking,' she accused him. 'How could it possibly know?'

For the next ten minutes, and with amazing patience, he taught her to cast, standing close behind her to advise her when she went wrong, and to her utter amazement she found the experience exhilarating.

'If you had told me a month ago that I would be standing on a riverbank hoping a salmon would swim past and gobble up my fly, I would never have believed you,' she told Elliott.

'I didn't know you a month ago,' he reminded her.

'You had just come to live here and you were an unknown quantity.'

Her heart lurched at the thought of all he had yet to know, but she would not let her unacceptable guilt spoil her day. One day out of all the years, she thought. It must be mine.

Elliott was so close that she could have turned and touched his cheek.

'Time to eat,' he said abruptly, casting his own fly into the water.

She went to prepare the picnic, opening the basket to spread a checked tablecloth she had brought for the purpose on a flat rock above the river, keeping her distance from the fishermen who were casting downstream. Her father was in his element, standing thigh-deep in the brown water, and Elliott, too, seemed engrossed.

When everything was in place, she walked along the bank towards them.

'Luncheon is served!' she announced gaily. 'No prize for who gets there first!'

The two men reeled in their lines, laying their rods carefully on the bank.

'Anything to declare?' she asked as her father came to stand beside her.

'Not a nibble!'

'I could have sworn I saw a dozen trout right under your nose,' she suggested, turning to Elliott. 'You haven't done too well yourself.'

'C'est la vie!' He laughed. 'We may do better later on. You can stand for hours without so much as a tug on your line, and then start pulling them in by the netful.'

'I hope you're right,' she responded. 'We need them for supper!'

They made their way up to the rocks to confront disaster—Amy was standing wide-eyed beside what remained of their lunch, while an enthusiastic pup polished off the last of the sandwiches.

'Duster must have been hungry,' Amy reflected.

Duster, his small stomach bulging, disappeared down the bank with a hang-dog expression which proved his guilt. It was impossible to do anything but laugh.

'That rather puts paid to our picnic,' Andrew Kennedy suggested, 'and just as I was feeling decidedly peckish!'

'There's more in the basket, but it's mostly cake,' Margot explained. 'That dog will have to be disciplined.'

Amy looked anxious.

'What will you do to him?' she wanted to know.

'Straight into the dog-house without any supper,' Margot decided. 'I thought collies were sensible creatures and wouldn't do a thing like that.' Her eyes, brimming with laughter, met Elliott's. 'You said he had an impeccable pedigree.'

'Which doesn't keep him from feeling hungry,' he declared.

Margot thought that she had never seen him looking so relaxed, so utterly carefree.

'If you'll all sit down,' she said, 'I'll see what's left in the basket.'

'If you'd given Duster another five minutes, I doubt if there would have been anything left, even the basket,' Elliott said. 'All dogs are thieves at heart.'

'And Duster is only a pup, after all,' she allowed, drawing a swift breath. 'At least he's proved his entertainment value. I've never seen a dog look so guilty!'

'They must have been delicious sandwiches,' he said.

The drama over, they sat down to what was left of the meal she had prepared so lovingly in the kitchen at Ottershaws, and even Amy found her tongue again to wonder where Duster had gone.

'He'll be sleeping it off in the bushes over there,'

Elliott told her, 'hoping to be forgiven when we've had time to think about it.'

Cathy came up, having checked the ponies.

'What's going on?' she wanted to know.

'Duster ate all the sandwiches,' Amy told her with a smile. 'We can only have cake now.'

'Like Marie Antoinette!' Cathy grinned. 'I thought that pup was up to no good.' She glanced from one of them to the other. 'Shall I ride back to the farm and get something more substantial?' she offered.

'We'll survive,' Elliott decided. 'At least Duster couldn't use a bottle-opener!'

Margot produced the lemonade and two bottles of wine.

'There's not much point in crying over spilt milk,' she pointed out, 'and at least we'll be hungry by supper-time.'

They ate what remained in the basket in blissful silence, washing the cake down with wine and lemonade, of which there was more than enough. After several minutes Margot was conscious of Cathy watching her with an odd sort of suspicion in her eyes, which somehow seemed to include Elliott. It wasn't too hard to put a name to that look, she thought. Cathy was jealous. Having been brought up from earliest childhood as 'the girl next door', Cathy had grown possessive, and while she still mourned Neil she now considered Elliott to be her personal property. Whether she saw him as Neil's successor, however, was another matter, but the fact seemed clear enough that resentment was already stirring in her impetuous heart.

It was all so pointless, Margot decided, because Elliott was patently not in love with anyone. He had decided against love or any other commitment while he sought his brother's betrayer.

Again her mind turned to the thought of Neil

Dundass. It was a name to conjure with, yet she was certain that she had never heard it before, although her first glimpse of Elliott on the narrow staircase of the factor's office in Galashiels had seemed vaguely familiar.

Dismissing it now as she had done then, she looked across the impromptu table to where Elliott was sitting beside her father. This is our day, remember, she said to herself. Be happy in it!

Yet it was to end in near disaster.

They gathered up the picnic things, stowing them back into the basket while the fishermen rested on the grass. Elliott lay sprawled out with his hands clasped behind his head, a picture of contentment, while her father drew lazily on his pipe, puffing little eddies of smoke into the air.

'Like Big Chief Sitting Bull!' Cathy joked. 'Where did you find a pipe like that?'

'In Austria. I thought it gave me a sort of rakish charm.' Andrew turned on his side to consider her. 'You're doing a lot for Amy, Cathy, and I appreciate it,' he told her more seriously.

'We like each other,' Cathy said. 'It's just a shame she has to be on her own.'

His face sobered at the reference to Amy's missing father.

'I'm hoping he will come back one of these days,' he said quietly. 'Then we can be a family again.'

Margot took up the thought. Today they had been like a big, happy family sharing the pleasures of a picnic beside the river, allowing all the other issues in life to pass them by, and even Cathy had admitted to a new interest when she had spoken about Amy. It could so easily come true, at least in part, and Ottershaws was hers for another three years.

Cathy dragged herself away to inspect the ponies.

'They don't like to be tied up for too long,' she

explained.

Andrew Kennedy tapped the remaining tobacco from his pipe as he rose to his feet.

'I'll have another go at the fish,' he said. 'There must be the odd unsuspecting trout somewhere.'

Elliott got up to follow him.

'I'll come, too,' Amy offered. 'I want to catch a fish.'

Elliott found an arched twig which had been shed from one of the overhanging trees, tying a piece of line to it for her inspection.

'It isn't a real rod,' she pointed out.

'It'll do,' he said, 'for the present. You're as likely to land a catch with it as any of us!'

'Don't go too near the pool,' Margot admonished. 'Stay up here in the shallows.'

'I'm going to fish!' Amy gloated. 'I'm going to catch a fish all by myself!'

She sat down on the riverbank while Margot gave her attention to the picnic basket, only looking up when she heard the splash.

Amy was in the water, floundering about, while the makeshift rod floated out of her reach. Every breath seemed to have been crushed out of Margot's body as she rushed across the stones to her rescue, but Elliott got there before her, making his purposeful way into the shallows to lift the dripping child into his arms.

'We wanted a fish and now we've got one,' he said quite calmly, wading back with her to the safety of the bank. 'We didn't expect such a big one, though, all dressed up as a little girl!'

All the fright vanished from Amy's face as he put her down on to her feet, and she struggled ahead of him up the bank.

'I'm a fish!' she announced uncertainly. 'Look at me, Aunty Margot! I'm a fish!'

Cathy came rushing down from the road.

'What's gone wrong?' She caught Amy into her

arms. 'You're all wet.'

Margot found her voice at last.

'It all happened so quickly.' She looked at Elliott. 'Too quickly for me,' she confessed. 'I have you to thank for saving her, Elliott.'

'She wouldn't have drowned,' he said quietly enough, 'but we had to make light of it because she was frightened. She was only in the shallows, but she must have had quite a shock.' He noticed her colourless face. 'So have you,' he added.

'Yes,' she had to admit. 'Thank heaven you were there at the right moment.'

He put a sympathetic hand on her arm.

'Sit down for a minute,' he advised. 'We'll have to get her home and into some dry clothes. She'll come to no harm.'

It was true. In the shelter of Cathy's arms Amy's confidence was fast returning.

'I could have caught a fish,' she protested. 'I could have done it!'

Hearing their voices Andrew Kennedy appeared from his stance farther down the river.

'What's all the commotion about?' he wanted to know.

'Amy fell in,' Cathy told him. 'Nobody was taking care of her.'

The unjust accusation stung Margot to a rejoinder.

'That's not quite true, Cathy,' she objected. 'It was an accident.'

Amy clung to Cathy's hand.

'I want to go home,' she said.

'And so you shall.' Andrew Kennedy looked at Elliott. 'Would you run them back in the Range Rover?' he asked. 'I'll clear up here and walk back. I think Margot should go with you right away.'

'Of course.' Elliott lifted Amy out of Cathy's arms. 'Time for a bath and a nice hot chocolate drink,' he

consoled, smoothing the wet hair back from her forehead. 'We'll get you a proper rod next time, with a real
fly on it. That's a promise!' he declared.

Margot's eyes met his over the wet curls, conscious
of a moment of comfort until confusion engulfed her
once more. The impulse to confess all to this man who
held Amy so tenderly, turning her frightened tears
into immediate laughter, was stronger than ever, but
how could she talk to him about Olivia Hallam and his
brother's downfall without this new friendship which
now existed between them breaking down irretriev-
ably? She had glimpsed the darker side of his nature
once or twice, aware of his resolve to face Olivia
Hallam with her treachery, and her heart lurched at
the prospect of the final confrontation which must
surely come.

'I'm ready to go,' she said, leaving Amy in the safety
of his arms.

She would tell him quite soon, she decided, but not
yet, not on this warm spring day with the sun high
above the Cheviot and the whole world seemingly at
peace.

'I suppose I'd better take the ponies back to the
Mains,' Cathy suggested ungraciously. 'They've been
standing around long enough.'

'Will you bring Brown Bess tomorrow?' Amy
wanted to know.

'Maybe we should have a day off tomorrow,' Cathy
decided, 'but I'll come the next day.'

Margot sat in the Range Rover with Amy on her
knee wrapped warmly in the picnic rug, and Elliott got
in and drove away, leaving Cathy to clear up the riverbank with Andrew Kennedy.

It was a short journey to Ottershaws.

'She doesn't seem to be any the worse for her dip in
the river,' Margot said.

'*She* would like some hot chocolate,' Amy

announced. 'Then *she* can go to bed.'

Elliott laughed.

'*She's* got her wits about her,' he remarked. 'I promised the hot chocolate.'

Margot smiled.

'We can't go back on your word. I just hope there's some chocolate in the house!'

When they drove up to Ottershaws, Mrs Daley met them at the door.

'There's been a gentleman phoning you from London,' she announced.

Henry, Margot thought.

'Did he give his name?'

'He said it didn't matter. He would phone again.' The housekeeper helped Amy down from the Range Rover. 'Goodness me!' she exclaimed. 'What happened to you?'

Margot looked at Elliott.

'You're soaked through,' she said. 'I'll give you something of my father's to change into.'

He shrugged.

'I'm used to getting wet,' he said. 'A quick dip in the river won't kill me.'

'But you will stay, at least to have that hot chocolate with Amy?'

While she was active there was no room for emotion, but when Amy was finally on her way upstairs, telling Mrs Daley all about her adventure, reaction set in. Elliott was standing at the dining-room window when she rejoined him with two mugs of steaming chocolate on a tray.

'I have so much to thank you for,' she said unsteadily. 'If anything had happened to Amy I would never have been able to forgive myself.'

'Nothing did happen.' He took the tray from her to set it down on the table. 'I think we came out of it very well.'

She turned away as sudden tears filled her eyes.

'It could have been much, much worse,' she said, her hands covering her face.

Gently he took her hands away, seeing the tears she could no longer hide.

'Margot, this isn't like you,' he said.

'Oh, I know—I know! I didn't mean to be so weak, only there were so many things——'

His hands slid up to her shoulders and suddenly he was holding her close. In ecstasy and agony she returned his kiss, forgetting everything in one blinding moment which blotted out the past, the future and what might become of them, leaving only the present for them to share.

He put her gently from him.

'Amy is safe,' he said, 'and now you must forget about it, as she has done. She sees it now as a big adventure, that's all.' He wiped a single tear from her cheek with his forefinger. 'Agreed?' he asked.

Agreed about Amy, she thought, but not about how she was to tell him the truth.

'Elliott,' she began hesitantly, 'I have something to say to you.'

'Not now,' he decided. 'You are overwrought. Tomorrow will do.'

She offered him a forlorn little smile as the telephone rang. Tomorrow or the day after, she thought; what did it really matter?

'Your friend from London,' he said, moving to the door. 'I think you'd better answer that. It might be important.'

When she lifted the receiver, she heard her brother's voice at the end of the line.

'Jamie!' she cried. 'Where are you?'

Elliott Dundass walked across the hall with a grim look on his face and a hint of disappointment in his eyes. The past had come to claim her.

Margot held on to the telephone receiver as if for support. Was this the answer to all her dreams for Amy?

'I'm in London,' James Kennedy told her. 'I arrived yesterday. I got your letter before I left Bahrain, giving me your address, but you know how I am about writing letters.'

'Yes, I know,' she admitted, her heart beating fast. 'But what now? Are you coming up here?'

There was a moment's pause, a hesitation of thought, before he answered her question.

'I guess it's the right thing for me to do,' he said.

'Certainly it is! We haven't seen you for over four years, Jamie, and Amy doesn't know you.'

'Ah, yes—Amy,' he said awkwardly. 'She must have grown.'

'Children do.' Margot swallowed hard. 'You have a very beautiful daughter here, Jamie, just waiting to see you. Why put the meeting off any longer?'

'How is the old man?' he asked, without answering the direct question. 'Still ready to dash off to the far ends of the earth at a moment's notice, or has he settled down at last?'

'I'll answer all your questions when you get here.' Margot was determined to be firm, not wanting to let this opportunity slip away from them. 'Look up trains and let me know when you are coming. Someone will be at Berwick to meet you.'

'The same old Margot!' he reflected. 'What took you so far away from London?'

'A virus,' she told him.

'But why Scotland?'

'I realise now that I had heard a lot about it from someone, although I can't quite recall who it was. Anyway, we're here and loving it,' she added eagerly. 'I think you will, too.'

'I've made a decision,' he said. 'No more Bahrain.'

'James, that's splendid! Will you come back here to work?'

'I've been offered a job,' he admitted. 'But we'll talk about it when we meet,' he added carefully.

'Jamie,' she said, 'I want you to come here. I want you to see Amy as she is now, a delightful, happy little girl who will shortly be going to school. Will you please come? Will you give yourself this chance?'

'I'll phone you,' he said slowly, 'as soon as I've looked up trains.'

She put down the receiver with a long drawn out sigh. She had won her point, and in spite of the fact that he had made no firm decision to take his daughter back into his life at least he was going to meet her.

Elliott had gone without her noticing, but soon her father had arrived and they were sharing the good news of his son's return.

'It's time Jamie was back in England,' he said. 'Time he had forgotten.'

'I don't think he'll ever forget Emily.'

'I didn't mean that, exactly.' Andrew put his rod down in the hall. 'What I should have said was that it was time he put the past behind him, where it belongs, and looked towards the future. He's had enough of Bahrain from what you've just told me, and that's not surprising. Working your guts out in a hot climate is all very well for a year or two, but you long for a breath of cold air in the end and the sun not beating you into the earth all day. You want to come home.'

'I wonder what he'll think of Ottershaws,' Margot said, looking round the raftered hall.

'That remains to be seen.' He gave her a quick look. 'If he decides to make other arrangements for Amy,' he suggested, 'it would leave you free.'

'Free?' She looked round at him in sudden confusion.

'Free to give everything you have to your career.' He spelled it out to her. 'You won't have a frog in your throat forever!'

'And I don't suppose I'll be at Ottershaws forever,' Margot said wistfully, 'but for now it's going to be the answer to a great many things. I feel sure of that, at least.'

James telephoned again the following morning, giving them the arrival time of his train.

'I'll go to Berwick,' her father offered. 'You'll want to stay here with Amy.'

'I think that will be best,' Margot agreed. 'Cathy can't be here, so we'll go for a walk on the moor. It may take Amy some time to adjust to the news.'

Amy, however, was quite complacent about it.

'Will he bring me a present?' she asked when she had considered her father's return for a thoughtful moment or two. 'Cathy said he would.'

'What else did Cathy say?' Margot asked as they went on to the moor.

'She said he was sure to come back one day, because fathers and little girls loved each other very much.'

Margot swallowed the lump in her throat.

'Sometimes Cathy can be very wise,' she said.

Without actually thinking about it, she took the track which led towards Sun Hill, meeting Elliott at the edge of the bluebell wood where he had stopped to watch the collies gathering in some sheep.

'I was planning to come down with a few books,' he said. 'I took them to Sun Hill a while ago, but I thought they might be useful to you in the library. They're mostly histories of the Borders and there's a Walter Scott. Have you read *The Heart of Midlothian*?'

'Years ago when I was at school, but I'd like to read it again now that I'm actually living here,' Margot said, looking about her at the surrounding hills. 'I feel all this has been building up over the years,' she confessed, 'making me want to come.'

'To see for yourself?' he suggested, his keen gaze

following hers. 'And what have you found?'

She drew a deep breath.

'Perfection, but I suppose it's really too early to say yet. It's like—getting to know someone. It doesn't all come together in a couple of weeks.'

Amy was watching the collies crouched before the gathered sheep.

'Could Duster do that?' she asked, holding the pup in her arms.

'He'd have to be trained properly first,' Elliott explained.

Amy considered the condition for a full moment before she said, 'My daddy's coming to stay.'

'Oh?' Elliott looked at Margot.

'He was on the phone when you left Ottershaws,' she told him, eyes shining.

'I thought it was someone from London trying to spirit you back there,' he admitted.

'No, that wouldn't happen unless——' She caught her breath. 'Unless I had to go,' she added quietly.

Amy was anxious about the collies.

'Are they tired?' she asked.

Elliott laughed.

'No,' he explained. 'They lie like that while they're waiting. Watch this!'

His commanding whistle brought Nellie and Ruff to their feet, ears pointed expectantly as the sheep moved slowly uphill.

'Will you come to the house?' Elliott asked unexpectedly.

'Yes, please!' Amy accepted eagerly. 'Duster could see his mother.'

'And I could collect the Walter Scott,' Margot smiled. 'My brother won't be here till late afternoon.'

'Will you collect him from Berwick?'

'No. My father agreed to go. I think he would like to see James first—a sort of man-to-man thing.' They walked off after the sheep. 'I know he wants James to settle down in England and look after Amy, but that's in the lap of the gods, I suppose, because he'll have several decisions to make.'

They climbed towards Sun Hill, where Amy and the collies were united in boisterous greeting outside the sheep pens, and once again Margot found herself helping to make tea in the tiny, inadequate kitchen with the sun pouring in through the one small window above the sink. It was familiar territory now, suitable enough for bachelor living, she supposed, but after Ottershaws it seemed very small.

'Will you always live here?' she asked, waiting for the kettle to boil.

Elliott shrugged.

'I haven't thought about it.' He found some biscuits to put on a plate. 'When your life changes dramatically, you tend to progress one step at a time.'

'Yes,' she agreed uncertainly, 'that's true.'

He had brought her back to thinking about the past.

'Elliott,' she said, 'I have something to tell you.'

He looked across the kitchen at her.

'Can it wait?' he asked. 'The kettle's on the boil!'

Amy was still in the garden playing with the dogs, but soon she would be rushing into the house asking for some milk and a biscuit. Margot decided that she had chosen the wrong moment to tell Elliott the truth.

He went ahead of her into the sitting-room when she had infused the tea, carrying it through on a tray, but when she followed him the dimness of the passageway after the sunny kitchen tripped her up. With a cry of alarm she stumbled on the step she had forgotten, leading from the kitchen into the passage, and she was on her hands and knees when Elliott reached her.

'What a fool I am!' she gasped. 'I should have remembered the step.'

'And I should have warned you.'

He picked her up, holding her in the semi-darkness of the passageway until their lips touched and he was kissing her passionately.

'Are you hurt?' he asked, at last.

'No—no, I'm all right!' She clung to him unbelievingly. 'Don't worry about it, Elliott. I shouldn't have been so careless.'

In the next moment all his tenderness had gone.

'What is it?' she whispered urgently.

'There is something I still have to do,' he said abruptly. 'I must go back to London.'

'Before you can tell me you love me?' She looked at him as he led her into the sitting-room, her eyes questioning.

'Before anything,' he said, as Amy came rushing through with the three dogs at her heels.

Margot drank her tea and rose to go. Someone was coming up the hill towards the house. It was Cathy.

'I didn't expect to find you here,' she said in her usual forthright way when she saw Margot at the door. 'Were you invited?'

'Not really,' Margot answered. 'We met Elliott when we were out walking and we came back with him. Amy was anxious to re-unite Duster with Nellie, I think.'

Cathy glanced at Elliott.

'I brought you some scones,' she told him. 'My mother's always concerned about you on baking days.'

'I'll never be out of her debt,' Elliott acknowledged absent-mindedly. 'Would you like some tea?'

Cathy didn't hesitate.

'I'll brew some coffee,' she said, obviously meaning to stay at least till his other visitors had gone.

Elliott walked with Margot to the gate.

'When will you go to London?' she asked huskily.

'In a day or two. I've had a letter from my brother's former flatmate which might make a difference to my way of thinking, though I can't be sure.'

coming because Aunty Margot told me.'

He held out his hand.

'Are you going to show me my room?' he asked.

Amy hesitated, eyes still fixed steadily on the brown ones which were so like her own.

'If you like,' she said unemotionally.

Margot stood back, allowing them to walk up the staircase ahead of her.

'What do you think?' she asked her father.

'Given time,' he decided, 'they will accept each other.'

'Children can be so unpredictable.' Margot sighed. 'I thought she might run off and not want to talk to him.'

'Curiosity might have something to do with it. She must often have wondered what he looked like, and you've always tried to keep his image alive,' Andrew reminded her.

Margot turned away.

'If he doesn't make an effort this time,' she said, 'I'll never forgive him.'

It was the start of a new endeavour which kept them all very much aware of the situation. The present of two Arabian dolls which James had brought for her delighted Amy, although she was far more interested in animals. When she had introduced him to Duster, she told him about her riding lessons on Brown Bess and how Cathy thought she might be able to have a pony of her own one day.

'And who might Cathy be?' James enquired, smiling broadly.

'She lives down at the Mains,' Amy explained, as if it shouldn't really be necessary, 'and she has lots and lots of ponies.'

'Her father breeds horses,' Margot translated, 'and Cathy runs a small riding-school.'

'Cathy appears to be a useful person to know,' James observed. 'Do you think she might be able to find me a horse to ride?'

'Maybe.' Margot was doubtful. 'It would be her father's decision, I suppose.'

'How old is Cathy?' was the next question.

'A very young twenty-year-old,' Andrew Kennedy put in. 'Most of her life has been spent at Lowther Mains, but that doesn't necessarily mean she's dull. On the contrary,' he added, pouring a whisky for his son, 'she's something of a firebrand, but she's a good little horsewoman and that's the main thing as far as Amy's riding lessons are concerned.'

The following morning, as was more or less inevitable, Cathy and James Kennedy met on the steps of Ottershaws. Cathy rode her own mount up the winding drive, leading the pony for Amy, and came to an abrupt stop when she saw the stranger on the steps outside the front door.

Margot had watched the meeting from the dining-room window, half-fearful of what Cathy might have to say, but when James came back into the house he was smiling.

'Firebrand was the right word for her,' he remarked, 'and she doesn't particularly like me.'

'That's because she's very fond of Amy,' Margot said. 'I hope she wasn't too rude.'

'We can't blame her for saying exactly what she thinks,' he mused. 'It would appear to be a childish characteristic she hasn't quite grown out of. She seems to be right for Amy, though, and that's the main thing.'

'Jamie,' Margot asked huskily, 'how long do you really mean to stay?'

'I've just put out a tender for a horse!'

'I meant that seriously,' she told him. 'Where do you intend to look for a job?'

He shrugged, considering her question for a moment before he answered.

'There's plenty of time, and I want to look around

first. I've had a tentative offer, but I'm not sure that it's exactly what I want.' He drew a deep breath. 'No more mistakes,' he added quietly. 'I've got a bit of money salted away and I have six months' holiday to take.' Suddenly he was looking deeply into her eyes. 'Could you bear with me for six months, do you think?'

'You don't have to ask.' A great surge of joy filled her heart. 'It will be wonderful for Amy—getting to know you.'

'I'll pay my way,' he offered, 'and do a few jobs around the place. Do we have to ask Dundass for permision to alter things?'

The mention of Elliott's name sent the colour flooding into Margot's cheeks, a fact which he was quick to observe.

'I don't think we'll have any trouble in that respect,' she said, 'but he's a very busy man. He lives up there on the hill, raising sheep.'

'Sheep?' he mused. 'I've always thought that might be a good life. I couldn't be doing with a job in the city. I'll scent around in the meantime, and no doubt I'll find my niche somewhere.'

'You won't go back to the Middle East?'

'I don't think so. How do I get in touch with this Dundass fellow to ask about building a new stable for the horse I just *might* be able to buy from Lowther Mains?'

'Elliott has been away.' Margot had thought of little else since their last meeting. 'He went to London a week ago, but he must be back by now.'

'Is he approachable?'

'Yes. I think you'll be able to plan your new stable without difficulty.'

Her heart was beating fast as she tried to picture exactly what had happened in London, what further information Elliott had managed to obtain. Of course, she should have told him who she was before he went there, but it was Elliott himself who had fended off her confession this time. He had taken her in his arms to comfort her and then he had kissed her passionately as if he never intended to let her go, but that was all forgotten when he put her aside, saying that he had something to do, something more important than telling her he loved her. Her heart contracted with a new and sudden pain. He must have returned to Sun Hill by now; he must be up there making the decision which could shatter their future for all time.

She didn't see him again for three days, days in which she went about the tasks she had allotted herself at Ottershaws; and she took James to Lowther Mains, where he bargained with Cathy's father for the horse Cathy had practically refused him, leading it away in triumph to the makeshift stable he had provided for it at Ottershaws.

When she saw Elliott on the hill just above the bluebell wood, leading a small flock of sheep, Margot went resolutely to meet him, thinking that she could no longer keep such pain to herself.

Climbing over the stile at the edge of the wood, she jumped down on to the grass road leading to the hill, and it seemed in that moment that they were alone in all the world, with only the sound of bleating sheep to distract them. When Elliott looked round at her, she had no need to ask the question which trembled on her lips.

'Did you find what you wanted in London?'

He came towards her, his eyes full of pain but empty of anger now.

'I found Olivia Hallam,' he said. 'I found this.'

He took a photograph from his breast pocket, thrusting it at her as she found herself looking into her own eyes.

'Elliott, please let me explain,' she cried. 'I sing under that name.'

'So I understand,' he returned harshly.

'Please listen to me!' she persisted, although he seemed to be surrounded by a wall of steel which she would never be able to penetrate however hard she tried. 'It was my mother's name. I took it when I began to sing professionally.'

He caught her by the shoulder, terrible anger returning to his eyes.

'Why did you come here?' he demanded. 'Why did you have to come, making me fall in love with you?' He searched her face, still condemning her. 'I thought I loved you—I wanted to love you.'

'And now?' she whispered, stricken by the haunted expression in his eyes.

'How can that be now that I know the truth?' he demanded. 'I have read the last of Neil's diaries.'

'What did you read?' she asked.

He thrust her from him.

'Do the details matter? The final thing is that my brother is dead because of you. He must have loved you, Margot—desperately—to have given up hope as he did, to have abandoned a whole bright future and all it might have held for him. How he must have loved you!'

'That's not true!' She heard her own voice, weakly protesting. 'I didn't even know Neil.'

'Don't lie to me!' He caught her arm. 'You were everything to him, all he ever wanted in a woman. He said so there in the diaries I was given by his flatmate. You were some sort of goddess as far as Neil was concerned—his idol.'

'With feet of clay,' she said bitterly, still trying to reach him to defend herself if she could. 'Elliott, I didn't know anyone called Neil Dundass.'

His fingers tightened on her arm.

'Perhaps you knew Nigel Grantley,' he suggested coldly. 'That was what Neil called himself, apparently, when he went to London to cry for the moon.'

She stood back, aghast, all the colour receding from her cheeks.

'Nigel?' she repeated. 'How could I have known? How could I have guessed that he was your brother? He never used any other name all the time I knew him, but I wasn't responsible for what happened to him. I never led him on or let him imagine that I was in love with him.' She looked deeply into his eyes, willing him to believe her, but she could see nothing there but distrust. 'How can you believe this of me,' she cried, 'if you really know me?'

'What else am I to believe?' he demanded.

She held her breath, looking down across the valley as she recognised his protective love for a younger brother who had fallen far short of his potential as far as Ottershaws was concerned.

'I think you should know the truth,' she said slowly, and curiously without hope. 'I didn't know Neil. I didn't know him at all in the way you mean. We were just ships that pass in the night, acquaintances with something in common. We were never lovers.'

'Do you expect me to believe that when he worshipped you?' he stormed, thrusting her away again. 'Don't lie any more, Margot—not now. I have been to London and I have found out the truth. Nothing will ever alter that.'

'Oh, Elliott!' She was looking at him as if she saw him through darkened glass, and her heart was suddenly cold. 'Nothing I can say will ever convince you now,' she whispered.

He saw hesitation in her eyes about the past, taking it for guilt.

'Nothing,' he repeated sternly. 'I shall always remember how it was.'

Striding off without another word, he left her to return to Ottershaws to rethink the future without him.

It was a future which might have held so much for them all, Margot thought, for Amy and her father and James if he could be persuaded to stay in Britain to bring up his daughter in love and companionship during the formative years of her young life, but now it all seemed to be falling apart before they had even discussed it in earnest.

When James went to Lowther Mains to pay for the mare he had bought, Margot went with him because Cathy and Amy were riding somewhere in the vicinity of the Mains with Cathy's other pupils, and she didn't want to be left alone to think about a future which held so many problems for them all.

Janet Graeme greeted them with genuine pleasure, glad, it seemed, that James had returned so quickly to honour his bargain.

'Cathy is out with her beginners,' she informed them, 'but she will be back soon. You'll wait and take a cup of tea?'

The aroma of newly baked bread drifted through from the farmhouse kitchen as they walked along the passageway towards a sun-filled sitting-room where a bright fire burned in the grate and well-worn armchairs stood invitingly around it. The Mains was old and warm and lived in, the sort of home Margot had longed to create, and James prowled around looking at everything, with his hands thrust deeply into his trouser pockets like a man content.

'I can't imagine you wanting to live anywhere else, Mrs Graeme,' he said. 'That's the thing about a family home—it has this air of solidarity you don't find anywhere else.'

'Three generations,' Janet Graeme told him proudly. 'We have only one regret,' she added slowly. 'There will be nobody to carry on the name once we are gone. Our only son was killed in an accident some years ago coming home from a rugby match in Edinburgh. It was a sore blow to us, as you can imagine, but Cathy has been everything we could expect in a daughter. Even more so,' she added, seeing Cathy approaching across the home fields with her retinue of ponies and young riders, who would disperse in the walled farmyard behind the house to go their separate ways.

Amy was with them, and for a moment Margot watched her through the window, entranced by the picture she saw. Far from being the shy, lacklustre little person she had been a few weeks ago, Amy was holding her own with the class of beginners, some of them more than double her age, and Cathy was watching her approvingly with the proprietorial smile Margot had noticed once or twice at Ottershaws. Cathy was pleased with the difference she had made in Amy's life in so short a time, and woe betide anyone who tried to disrupt it!

When she finally came into the sun-bright parlour, she seemed to challenge James Kennedy's presence there.

'Hello, Cathy,' he said, nothing daunted. 'What's new?'

She put her riding-crop down on the table nearest the door.

'We can't have something new to distract us every day of the week,' she told him distantly. 'At least, not up here. The class is doing very well, thank you, and especially Amy. I'm very proud of her progress.'

'I'm glad she's not afraid of a horse,' James said. 'I hope to take her out with me whenever I can.'

Cathy bridled at the suggestion.

'I'd get used to Clarinda first, if I were you,' she advised. 'She's not an easy mare to live with until she's completely sure of you, and the ponies irritate her at times.'

James endeavoured to conceal a smile.

'I know a lot of people like that,' he assured her, 'but

I dare say I'll be able to cope in due course.'

'Just remember that I warned you,' Cathy emphasised, 'for Amy's sake.'

'I'll do that.' James was looking at her closely, trying to probe beneath the surface antagonism that he had encountered at their very first meeting. 'I won't interfere with your training, Cathy,' he promised. 'You can be assured of that.'

'If I thought you were going to interfere, I'd give Amy up immediately,' Cathy retorted. 'You are paying for my tuition and Amy must obey the rules like everybody else.'

Janet Graeme looked across the room at her daughter in some surprise.

'Cathy is a very good teacher,' she remarked reassuringly. 'Good, and patient with children, but she doesn't do with interference. I tell her sometimes that she's too autocratic, but she says she needs to be, otherwise they would take advantage. You needn't worry about your daughter, Mr Kennedy. She'll do very well with Cathy.'

'I'm sure,' James said, accepting a newly baked scone from the plate she offered him. 'And I'm not worried in the slightest,' he added, meeting Cathy's hostile stare. 'I'm sure Cathy will be good for Amy, whatever she does.'

Amy came in, rosy-cheeked and full of excitement to report to their unexpected visitors.

'We went miles and miles,' she explained. 'Down over the river and up on to the moor past Sun Hill, an' we saw Mr Dundass, an' Nellie an' Ruff.'

Janet Graeme paused as she poured out the tea, looking at her daughter expectantly.

'What did Elliott think of London?' she asked. 'It's the second time he's been there in the past few weeks, and it isn't at all like him to be gallivanting away from Sun Hill so soon after the lambing.'

'I don't think he was gallivanting, exactly,' Cathy answered, helping to pass the teacups. 'He had something important to do.'

Margot felt a lump rising in her throat, wondering exactly what Elliott had told Cathy about their encounter on the moor. Surely, surely he couldn't have confided in Cathy or anyone else what he had said to her in anger and despair?

'We only saw Elliott from a distance,' Cathy said. 'He was involved with the sheep.'

'You know you are always welcome at Sun Hill,' her mother reminded her, adding in an aside to Margot, 'They were all brought up together—Elliott and his brother and Cathy and Bruce, and of course we thought——'

'Nobody is interested in what might have been, Mother,' Cathy interrupted her abruptly. 'Not now. Neil is dead and Elliott is going his own way up there at Sun Hill. We're no longer children, and you have to recognise that. Elliott doesn't need to be taken care of any more than I do. We must make our own decisions and our own mistakes, like everybody else.'

'That's true,' Janet agreed, 'but if we could spare you heartache we would. Is your father settled down at Ottershaws, Miss Kennedy?' she asked, changing the subject because Margot looked uneasy. 'I saw him fishing along the river yesterday and he seemed a contented man.'

'He's there today again.' Margot smiled. 'We've got more fish than we'll need for the next month. Could we bring you some down?' she asked spontaneously, glad of this new, blossoming friendship which seemed to include them all. 'James would be only too willing to ride down with a salmon now and then if your husband is too busy to fish.'

'A farmer is always busy,' Janet assured her, 'and a salmon now and then would be more than welcome.'

She glanced questioningly in James's direction. 'Is this a kind of holiday for you?' she asked.

'I guess I'll be here for most of the summer,' he told her, looking coolly in Cathy's direction. 'I have to get to know my daughter, you see.'

A great surge of joy lifted Margot's heart. This was wonderful news, coming as it did in such an unexpected way.

Cathy was standing beside the door, waiting for them to go.

'Can you take Amy home?' she asked. 'It would save me the double journey.'

'Why not?' James agreed. 'We have Margot's car and there's only the two of us. What's the programme for tomorrow, by the way?' he added easily. 'Another riding lesson?'

'Not tomorrow.' Cathy pushed her hair back from her face. 'Amy is only a beginner, and we're practising for the gymkhana in a few weeks' time. It's too early for her to go for the jumps yet.'

'I don't want her to do anything too dangerous,' James agreed unexpectedly, 'and you're the boss. What you say goes as far as Amy is concerned.'

'I'll pick her up on Thursday,' Cathy promised, almost reluctantly. 'If she's available.'

There was a decided twinkle in James Kennedy's eyes as he came level with her.

'Would you object to another pupil?' he enquired. 'I'm not quite sure whether I can handle the mettlesome Cassandra—or is it Clarissa?—on my own terms, and I'd like to see how Amy is progressing.'

'You bought *Clarinda*,' Cathy corrected him, 'but perhaps you don't know your Burns. I've already told you how well Amy is doing, but come if you like.' A bright colour stained her cheeks. 'There's no charge for a ride across the moor.'

Her father came to the back door as they were

leaving.

'There was no hurry for the cheque,' he told James. 'The mare was needing exercise, and I'm glad she's not going too far away. She's used to these parts, and I have to confess I don't like parting with my horses once I've reared them.'

'We'd have the stables full of them if he had his way!' his wife laughed. 'Come back as often as you can,' she added. 'We like a visitor.'

Short of sending them back to Ottershaws with a parcel of freshly baked scones, Janet was treating them as friends already, although she reserved her closest affection for Elliott Dundass. Perhaps Cathy would go up to Sun Hill with the freshly baked scones they had left, telling Elliott that they had been to the Mains.

Margot thought of Elliott constantly, aware that she might see very little of him in the future, although they lived such a short distance apart. Still shocked by the revelation that Nigel Grantley and his brother were one and the same person, she forced her mind back to her first meeting in London with Nigel. In a good many ways she had taken him under her wing at first, introducing him to this one and that because he had seemed lonely; but gradually she had become aware of his obsession for her, which in so many ways was part of his overwhelming desire to succeed. Her own apparent success had blinded him to everything else, and very soon he had been living on her doorstep, begging introductions to agents, seeking advice, following her everywhere. Henry Levitt had called him an embarrassment and possibly Henry had been right, as he was right about most things, but she had not been able to tear herself away. There had been something about Nigel which she had liked, a little-boy appeal which had touched her sensitive heart, even though she was fully aware of all the ruthlessness around them. Then, quite suddenly, he had become arrogant and more sure of himself than he needed to be. He saw success everywhere he looked, and was determined to achieve it for himself without anyone's help.

At that stage she had been deeply engrossed in her own career and they had lost sight of each other, going their separate ways, and she had completely forgotten about the little incident which had so distressed her until someone had told her that Nigel was dead, killed in an accident because he had been driving too fast in an old car. He had achieved nothing. His life had been like a light extinguished soon after it was lit, a brief, bright flame burning itself out on the altar of ambition when he had very little talent to sustain it.

Now it had all come round full circle when she had been faced with a crisis of her own. Knowing that she had to get away from London for a while, a picture had formed in her mind of green hills and far-away places, a word picture which was not difficult to trace back to Nigel's descriptions of his native land. It had been there in her mind waiting to be used when she needed it, and although she had not connected it with Nigel at the time she knew now that it had influenced her final choice to come to the Border country to see for herself.

It was all too difficult to believe for a moment, too much like a dream when she thought how easily she had fallen in love with Elliott Dundass. Surely she could explain this to him? Surely he would understand?

Yet she had tried to explain, begging him to understand, but he had turned away in anger and perhaps contempt.

When she looked up towards Sun Hill she felt that she had been waiting for him at Ottershaws for a lifetime, yet she saw him the very next day from her bedroom window, striding up the drive towards the house with a look of purpose about him which was evident even at that distance.

Her heart racing, she ran down the broad staircase to

the front door, wrenching it open to let in the sunshine, but he was nowhere to be seen. Her heart dropped like a stone. He had come to see someone else.

In a moment or two she heard voices at the gable end of the house, Elliott's and her brother's voice in friendly greeting. She went slowly out into the garden, walking towards them, a fixed smile on her lips to cover the memory of their last meeting.

'Elliott has come about the stable conversion,' James explained. 'I have to convince him that it's really necessary when we may need it for so short a time.'

The last few words had been Elliott's. She knew that, but she also knew he wasn't prepared to take back a single word he had said to her at their last meeting. He believed her guilty, and nothing she could say would ever alter the fact, not if she pleaded with him for a hundred years!

Suddenly there was something else. If she told him the truth about his brother and how he had lived when he saw the success he coveted so much slipping away from him, she would destroy something Elliott had cherished for so long, a brotherly love which had embraced Ottershaws and all it had stood for over the years.

'Perhaps something temporary can be arranged,' she found herself saying, her voice seeming to come from some great distance as they stood there contemplating the inadequate stable building. 'I don't want to change Ottershaws, Elliott, not in any way, so that's why it must be your decision.'

He looked round at her, thinking about Amy.

'James tells me he wants to buy Amy a pony of her own,' he said briefly. 'That will mean another separate stable, because Clarinda isn't too reliable and a pony might irritate her. We had several loose-boxes at one time when my brother was alive, but they've been put to other use, as you can see. Maybe,' he decided, 'one of them could be cleared out and used for the pony.'

'It's a thought,' James agreed, 'but the pony isn't an established fact yet. I've told Amy she must wait for her next birthday and we'll see.'

'It will give her a lot of pleasure,' Elliott said, 'and she's old enough to look after it on her own now with a friendly word of advice from whoever happens to be around.'

'Which will mean Cathy,' James predicted, smiling at the thought. 'I guess she will be as enthusiastic about the pony as Amy herself.'

'I'd have to be quite sure that it was even-tempered,' Margot submitted. 'I'm not willing to take a chance with Amy now that she's become so headstrong.'

'I won't have her wrapped in cotton wool,' James objected. 'I want her sturdy and strong and willing to take a chance.'

At long last he was taking a positive interest in his daughter, and Margot's heart glowed with pleasure. This was what she had always wanted, and already it was in her grasp. Amy would have a real father at last, and not some vague, shadowy figure in the background of her life who could never seem truly real.

Amy came running through the shrubbery, pausing for a moment when she saw them standing by the stable door.

'Not a word about the pony,' James cautioned under his breath. 'Otherwise we'll hear nothing else till she gets it!'

Amy took her father's hand.

'Can you come and see what I've been doing?' she asked. 'I've made a kennel for the pup.'

'My goodness!' James exclaimed. 'I wondered where you had been all morning and what all the hammering was about.'

Amy took Elliott into her confidence.

'It's not a very good kennel,' she confessed. 'Not like

the one you have for Telfer at Sun Hill, but it was all the wood I could find.'

James's eyebrows shot up.

'I wonder what has suffered in the process,' he remarked in a brief aside to their visitor. 'I'd better go and see.'

As Margot watched, Amy led her father round the gable end of the house; the man of strength and the little child who trusted him.

'I'm so glad of that,' she said as Elliott turned to go back down the drive. 'Amy needs her father more than ever now that she is growing up and mixing with other children. Perhaps she lived too sheltered a life in London among so many older people. My father was away a great deal and I tried to cope as best I could, but an aunt can never be a real substitute for a mother.'

'You took on a lot when you offered to take care of her,' he observed, walking slowly by her side. 'Her mother died, I understand, when she was very young.'

'Not long after she was born. It shattered James, I'm afraid. They were so very much in love, you see, and he wouldn't look at Amy just at first because he blamed her for Emily's death.'

'I can understand how he felt.' Suddenly his mouth was grim. 'But surely he has come to his senses now? Amy is a delightful child.'

'My father and I are hoping that this will be the final answer,' she confessed. 'It was the main reason why we came to Scotland, and now it seems to be working out for Amy and James, at least.'

'And you?' he asked almost stiffly. 'What will you do if your brother decides to settle in Britain and look for a job? Will you pick up the threads and go happily back to your successful career in music?'

'I don't know,' she answered carefully. 'I have no career, as such, at the moment, but I will certainly have to go back to London in the near future for a final check-up in Harley Street. My voice has come back almost one hundred per cent, but it will have to be put to a final test. Perhaps then I can make a decision.'

Her voice had faltered over the last few words, husky again with sudden emotion.

'I wish we had something to say to each other, Elliott,' she said. 'I wish we could talk this thing out and try to understand one another.'

He stopped in his tracks, looking down at her in the dappled sunshine of the tree-lined drive.

'I came here to ask you to go,' he said harshly. 'To leave Ottershaws for good, but now I have changed my mind. Your family is too greatly involved—Amy and James and your father—and we made a bargain. I will keep my part of it.'

'And I mine.' She could hardly speak for the tears choking against her throat. 'But couldn't we continue to be neighbourly, at least?'

He shook his head.

'A neighbour is someone you have known for a long time whom you can turn to in an emergency, knowing you wouldn't be let down,' he said coldly. 'Someone you can trust.'

'How can we live like that?' she cried. 'Breathing the same air, seeing each other day by day, but trying to avoid each other?'

'I've no doubt we can find a way,' he said, his eyes dark with pain. 'If you are going back to London, the problem will be solved for you, at least.'

She watched him go, walking away with that long, loping stride she had come to recognise even from a distance, walking out of her life for ever, perhaps.

Yet she was to meet him again two days later, and all because of Amy.

Elspeth Daley came to the back door as she returned from the village, where she had gone to post some letters.

'I thought you had the wee one with you,' she remarked.

'Amy?' Margot looked about her at the deserted garden. 'It seemed a long way to ask her to walk in all this sudden heat.'

Elspeth looked concerned.

'I haven't seen her for over an hour. She was playing with that pup of hers down by the shrubbery when I came in to put the dinner on. She could be with your brother, though,' she suggested. 'Or with Mr Kennedy.'

'My father is fishing,' Margot said. 'She wouldn't go down to the river by herself. Where is James?' she asked with a sudden edge in her voice.

'He took that mare of his out an hour ago to ride to the Mains,' Elspeth informed her. 'It strikes me he's never away from there these days!'

Margot hurried down through the garden towards the shrubbery, thinking that Amy couldn't be too far away. She had been warned about going alone on to the moor and normally she was an obedient child, but, call as Margot might, there was no immediate reply. Not even an excited bark, Margot reflected, knowing that where Amy went the pup would surely follow.

When she reached the shrubbery gate she found it standing open. Amy, she thought, you're growing far too adventurous!

Skirting the edge of the wood where the wild hyacinths made a blue carpet beneath the trees, she looked out across the moor to the low barrier of the foothills where Elliott Dundass grazed his flock, but there was no sign of anyone there save the distant sheep.

Hurrying, she reached the moor road, aware suddenly of excited barking on the other side of the dry-stone wall which bounded it. Certainly that was the pup, and Amy must be there, too. Half angry and half relieved, she reached the five-barred gate which would give her a better view, and what she saw brought a reluctant but relieved smile to her lips. Amy was standing less than a hundred yards away, watching the antics of the young Border collie as he bounded across the moor in pursuit of a group of lambs who had been playing in the shelter of the wall and were now scattering towards their alarmed mothers some distance away. She called out sharply and, true to generations of breeding, the young collie crouched down on the grass to move slowly forwards towards the advancing ewes.

'Amy, get out of the way!' Margot shouted, although there was really very little immediate danger. 'Call Duster off. He's frightening the sheep.'

When Amy called him, the pup took very little notice, till a sharper, more insistent whistle stopped him in his exuberant tracks. A man had come up from the far side of the wall, walking with a long, easy stride which was instantly recognisible. Elliott had heard the excited barking and had come to investigate.

He came towards them as Amy ran to rescue the pup. Margot tossed the windblown hair back from her forehead.

'Elliott, I'm sorry!' she apologised. 'I had no idea Amy had come this far, and I've warned her about the lambs. I hope there isn't any damage.'

'Only alarm,' he said, looking down at her in the way that made her heart turn over. 'The lambs possibly think it's some sort of game, but the ewes could turn nasty. It's the protective mother instinct, I suppose.'

'Amy will have to learn,' she said. 'I wouldn't want her to appear disobedient, especially when she will soon be going to school.'

'You've made up your mind about that?' he asked.

'Keeping her here?'

'Yes.' She drew a deep breath. 'It's what will be best for her in the long run.'

Amy came towards them, the reluctant pup close at her heels.

'Duster didn't mean to hurt the lambs,' she explained, looking up at Elliott, her enormous eyes filled with apology. 'He only wanted to play with them and he's very sorry,' she added sorrowfully.

'I quite believe he is,' Elliott answered, kneeling down beside her so that he could make his point, eye to eye. 'But the thing is, Amy, good sheepdogs have to be trained properly. They have to understand about the sheep and answer to a command immediately. I had to train Nellie to do that when she was a pup like Duster, and now we must teach Duster to behave properly on the hill. It won't take very long,' he promised, 'and I think he will be as good as his mother one day.'

Amy's eyes were round with wonder as she put in a word for her pet.

'He is really a very good dog,' she said solemnly. 'He doesn't dig up the flowerbeds any more and he sleeps in his kennel all night now without crying.' Suddenly she was reminded of the pup's mother. 'Could we go and see Nellie, please?' she asked, putting a trusting hand into his as he straightened. 'We're very near your house,' she pointed out hopefully.

'Amy!' Margot protested, but Amy had already made her point.

'Why not?' Elliott said. 'Do you think you can walk that far?'

'I'm very good at walking,' Amy told him. 'I can walk anywhere.'

Elliott looked round at Margot.

'It's up to you,' he said.

He thought she wouldn't want to go to Sun Hill again, Margot realised, but how could she possibly refuse? To Amy it was such an important request, and her own foolish heart was insisting, just once more!

She turned towards the stone-built cottage on the hill above them, thinking how lonely it looked, standing there by itself, waiting for a visitor.

'We mustn't stay very long,' she decided. 'Mrs Daley was preparing the dinner when we came out.'

Elliott glanced at his watch.

'I've left mine in the oven,' he said. 'Eternal stew!'

They climbed the hill with Amy between them chattering about Cathy and the ponies and the other children who were part of the riding-school; a man and a woman and a little girl whose life was suddenly full of happiness. The perfect family, Margot thought, the thing she would have loved for herself above all other.

When they reached Sun Hill, Nellie rushed to meet them, fussing over her offspring and his new mistress as if they had never been parted.

'She remembers!' Amy marvelled. 'She's licking Duster all over!'

'Will you come in?' Elliott asked half reluctantly.

'I'd like to stay here—out in the sun,' Margot said, knowing that she was about to make one last appeal for his friendship. 'That's how I've always thought of this place,' she added unsteadily. 'Wrapped up in sunshine.'

'You're seeing it at its best,' he told her as Amy ran with the dogs round the gable end of the house. 'In winter it can be very bleak and less than friendly.'

'I know you must miss Ottershaws,' she said. 'It is such a sheltered house.'

He looked down towards the bluebell wood.

'It's far too big for one man and three dogs,' he said

decisively.

'You'll marry one day,' she suggested. 'Then you will need Ottershaws back again.'

He leaned forward against the low, dry-stone wall which separated the cottage from the moor.

'I hardly think so,' he said. 'It's a matter of hard cash, and I'm content as I am.'

She saw the sunlight on the rolling hills all around them and heard the bleating of the sheep, knowing that he was speaking the truth up to a point. Beyond contentment lay the country of the heart which he was unwilling to explore.

'If ever you want Ottershaws back,' she offered, 'you have only to ask.'

He straightened, looking beyond her to his present home.

'That won't happen,' he said. 'I told you the other day that I would keep our bargain, and I meant it. Until you want to break the lease for a reason of your own, Ottershaws is yours.'

He was offering her nothing more than the bargain they had already made, but she wasn't prepared to accept that.

'Elliott,' she said, 'couldn't we start again? Couldn't we wipe the slate clean and try to forget the past?'

She knew he would refuse even before she had finished her desperate plea for his friendship, at least.

'You're asking me to forget Neil,' he said harshly, 'and that's something I could never do. He was my brother.'

Finality had been in every word, and she turned away from him with the tears she mustn't shed gathering in her eyes. The sunshine bathing the hills in golden light seemed like a mockery now as she watched the clouds gathering in the west, etching dark shadows on the hills. How could she ever reach him after this? He had made his decision and there was no more she could do about it unless she was prepared to destroy the faith he had always had in Neil.

'I think I understand,' she said slowly as he turned away.

Amy and the pup came rushing from the back of the house.

'We've had a long talk with Nellie,' she announced, 'and she thinks Duster should learn better manners.' She put a trusting hand into Elliott's. 'She thinks I should come here more often to have Duster trained properly.'

Margot's heart felt quite dead as she waited for Elliott's reply.

'I'll do my best, Amy,' he said. 'It takes a long time to train a sheepdog—the best part of two years if he's as frisky as Duster. He has to learn to gather the sheep without hurting or frightening them, you see, and we have to be patient with him at first.'

His tenderness towards the child was another part of his nature, a part she hadn't seen before, and suddenly Margot turned away.

'Don't let Amy persuade you against your will,' she said huskily. 'We really have no need for a trained dog at Ottershaws when we haven't any sheep.'

'My daddy's going to have lots of sheep one day,' Amy enlightened them unexpectedly. 'He said so, if he can get somewhere near here to live.'

The information surprised Margot, although she could not bring herself to think about the future at that moment.

'We must go,' she excused herself to Elliott. 'Thank you for being so understanding about the pup.'

He walked with them to the gate, holding Nellie

back when she would have followed them on to the moor.

'It was nice to go there, wasn't it?' Amy asked. 'I like Sun Hill very much.'

CHAPTER SIX

IN the weeks that followed, Elliott seemed to avoid them, working at Sun Hill as if the village and Ottershaws were in a different world. Margot saw him quite often at a distance, always with Nellie or the Labrador at heel, striding out across the moor with that powerful gait which she had come to recognise as part of the man, strong and determined, knowing the way he wanted to go. That way was never likely to cross her path again if he could possibly help it, she supposed. Ruthless in his decision once it had been made, he would keep to the letter of his vow. He would never forgive her for deserting his brother in his hour of need.

If only she had been able to get through to him, she thought bleakly; if only she could tell him the truth, but that truth was denied her because she knew what it would do to him. When she tried to persuade herself that she owed no real loyalty to Neil Dundass, it only brought her back to Elliott, to the disillusionment and pain she would inflict by freeing herself from guilt.

Once or twice she thought of discussing the problem with James, but she seldom caught him alone for more than five minutes at a time. He was carving out a niche for himself at Ottershaws, and all she could do was applaud. The mare he had bought was a constant source of pleasure to him, and he was often at Lowther Mains either 'blethering' to Janet and her husband or chatting up Cathy, who invariably tried to ignore him.

'Cathy's too bright not to see through you,' Margot

told him on one occasion. 'She can spot flattery a mile away!'

'It isn't all flattery,' he returned, suddenly serious. 'She could be the sort of person I admire.'

'If?' she asked, immediately interested.

'If she could curb that temper of hers a bit. Cathy's far too impetuous, like a squib going off as soon as you've put a match to it.'

'Which is no reason why you should carry a box of matches in your jacket pocket whenever you are likely to meet her,' Margot pointed out. 'Cathy may be over-sensitive at times, but I think she's genuine enough—and very loyal,' she added in all fairness to their impulsive neighbour.

'I don't dispute the loyalty bit,' he decided. 'That's admirable, but, when you become obsessed with an idea, that can be difficult, even at Cathy's age.'

'You're thinking about Neil Dundass,' she said slowly. 'I thought perhaps she was getting over him a little, clinging more to Elliott.'

'Cathy doesn't cling,' he said. 'That would never do! She's her own person and there's an end to it. But Elliott Dundass is a different proposition. I don't think he'll marry Cathy—or anybody else—while he has still so much to do at Sun Hill.'

'If that was his only reason——' Margot began, and then decided to keep her thoughts to herself. 'He works very hard at Sun Hill,' she agreed, her voice husky as always when she spoke about the man she loved so desperately. 'If I didn't know him so well I'd say he had taken on far too much trying to run the place on his own. He's out on the moor all day long, and sometimes I wonder when he eats—and what.'

'He ought to have a housekeeper,' James agreed, 'but he tells me he manages to muddle through and quite likes the freedom of doing his own thing. Mrs Graeme has the same thoughts about him as you

have,' he added briefly. 'I'm thinking about all those
scones she sends up with Cathy.'

'Elliott can't live on scones alone! He could be
neglecting himself,' Margot protested.

'Try telling him that!' her brother laughed. 'He would
be astounded, because he knows how to cook a salmon
straight out of the river and make a reasonable cup of
tea.'

'All right!' Margot agreed. 'I know he's independent
and wouldn't want to accept help even if he needed it,
but that could all be taken too far—like Cathy's
idealism.'

'I've asked him to come down here whenever he feels
like it,' James remarked unexpectedly.

Margot swung round to face him.

'And what did he say?' she asked.

'He hadn't time at the moment.'

Her heart sank, because it was the answer she had
expected. Elliott wouldn't come to Ottershaws because
she was there.

'How often have you gone to Sun Hill?' she asked.

'Often enough,' her brother told her. 'I stop there
occasionally when I'm riding back over the moor road
and we yarn about sheep. Elliott is a fountain of
knowledge in that respect.'

'And you are more than interested. Jamie,' she asked,
'is that what you want to do—buy some land and settle
near here?'

He thought for a moment before he answered her
weighted question.

'I've been thinking seriously about it, I must confess,'
he agreed.

'That would be wonderful!' She was thinking of
Amy. 'We'd all be together again, but you would have
a place of your own which Amy could really call home.'

'I've considered that, too,' he said, 'but it will all take
time, I guess. Rome wasn't built in a day, or something

of the sort, but I also have to think about you.'

'Why me?'

'Because you've given up so much of your time to look after Amy. Margot,' he added quickly as she would have protested, 'I know you haven't grudged a moment of it, but the time has come for me to shoulder my responsibilities in that respect, at least. I've come to know Amy quite well and I think we could get along together. It's a big step for a man, taking on a four-year-old daughter with a decided will of her own, but I reckon I ought to be able to do it—with a little bit of help.'

'From Cathy?' she asked doubtfully.

'From everyone,' he said. 'Cathy is very fond of Amy and my daughter adores her.'

'They have a lot in common,' Margot agreed, wondering where his confidence in Cathy might lead him if she was still deeply attached to Elliott. 'They were kindred souls right from the beginning.'

'It's like a fever,' he mused whimsically. 'This love of horseflesh. You either catch it or you don't. Maybe we should call it love at first sight!'

'I didn't think you were so romantic,' she observed, 'and they didn't hit it off completely at first glance. Cathy took her time to consider Amy, but eventually she gave in.'

'My daughter has everything it takes!' he acknowledged, preparing to ride away. 'Charisma, enthusiasm and amazing powers of persuasion. You must have encouraged her!'

'I did my best,' Margot assured him, watching as he rode towards Sun Hill.

She wasn't surprised that James and Elliott should have become friends when they had so much in common, she told herself. Only a little bit envious.

Amy began to follow her father everywhere, especially when Cathy was not available, and when he

finally bought her the promised pony on her fifth
birthday her joy knew no bounds. It was small and
honey-coloured, with a long, fine tail which stretched
nearly to the ground, and inevitably they called it
Honey, although its registered name was Firebrand.
Anything less mettlesome would have been hard to
imagine, and Margot's mind was at rest in that
respect, at least. When Cathy wasn't available, Honey
and her small delighted mistress followed James and
Clarinda all over the moor, riding carefully in all
weathers, like good companions with a common love.

How often they ended up at Sun Hill or met Elliott
on their travels it was difficult to say, but Amy began
to talk more and more about sheep and so it was easy
enough to guess that the two men had been discussing
the future in earnest.

'Buying land around here is going to be the most
difficult part,' James confessed one evening as they sat
over their after-dinner coffee in the sun-lounge
attached to the dining-room which had once been a
sizeable conservatory. 'People hang on to land in these
parts for grim death, I gather, so I'll be lucky to get
even an acre or two.'

'No chance of sharing the grazing at Sun Hill?' his
father asked, putting up his feet on a handy stool.
'Dundass must have plenty to spare.'

'I don't think he would even consider it,' James said.
'It's family land and that means a lot to him.'

Margot crossed to the window to look out.

'I hope you won't go too far away,' she said. 'I
wouldn't like to lose Amy altogether.'

'You won't be able to do that,' James assured her.
'Ottershaws will always be her second home.'

'For a while,' Margot agreed. 'You see,' she added,
her voice suddenly full of tears, 'I don't know how
long I'll be able to stay here.'

'Because of your career?' James asked. 'We all

understand that, Margot, and we can't stand in your way, but I thought——'

She turned, looking at him fiercely.

'You thought I wanted to stay here forever!' she cried. 'Well, I did in the beginning, but all that has changed now. I think—I think you can get on very well without me!'

The unexpected outburst kept them silent for a moment, wondering what had happened to precipitate such an explosion, until Andrew Kennedy said quietly, 'You know that isn't true, m'dear. We haven't made too great a show of it in the past, I must confess, but we do appreciate you and we want to see you happy.'

'I could have been happy here,' she said, immediately ashamed of her sharp rejoinder, 'but that's impossible now, especially in the long term. We don't belong, I expect. We're not exactly natives.'

Her father looked concerned at the bitterness in her tone.

'I haven't found that at all,' he said thoughtfully. 'Everybody—the Graemes and Elliott Dundass particularly, have gone out of their way to be helpful, and certainly Elliott has been more than accommodating about any alterations we have wanted to make. Take the stables, for instance——'

'I know! I know!' Margot was instantly ashamed of her emotional outburst. 'I suppose it's me, really. I'm restless and easily upset.'

'Which isn't like you,' Andrew Kennedy observed, looking at her closely. 'Are you fretting about your voice, about not being able to go on with your career?'

'There's that, of course.' Margot turned back to the window. 'Sooner or later I'll have to make a decision.' Her eyes were full of tears. 'I can't stay here doing nothing for ever.'

James thought he was being helpful when he said,

'Don't worry about us now that I've decided to
settle down in Britain. We'll get by, and you've done
more than enough already. I thought the other day
that we should get someone in to look after the house
permanently—a housekeeper of sorts who would live
in—and then you wouldn't feel so tied. You could
come and go whenever you liked.'

Margot blinked back the tears.

'We have Mrs Daley, and I think we could persuade
her to live in if there was an emergency. She's blunt
but very honest, the kind of person one could trust.'

It was all boiling down to trust and neighbourliness,
she thought harshly, the two attributes Elliott had
rejected when she had suggested them. No matter
how she might try to convince him, she had heard his
final word.

'When do you go to London for your check-up?' her
father asked at breakfast the following morning.

'At the end of the month. Mr Carlton should know
by then if there's any chance of getting my voice back
to full pitch. It means a lot to me,' she added
deliberately. 'After all, it could be my entire future.'

James paused at the door on his way out.

'I'm taking Clarinda,' he announced, 'and Amy
wants to come with me.'

'You will take care?' Margot cautioned. 'I don't trust
that mare of yours.'

'She's as good as gold now,' James assured her,
'and Amy will be on her own this morning. Cathy is
taking her advanced class over the jumps and I don't
think Amy should go to watch. It might put too many
ideas into her head.'

'Honey isn't ready for a gymkhana yet,' Margot
agreed, glad to see the interest he was now taking in
his daughter. 'But do be careful. I don't want to sound
like a clucking mother-hen, but the moors have been

out of bounds for Amy and Honey unless Cathy is with her.'

'I'll not even canter,' James promised with a twinkle in his eye. 'We'll walk all the way.'

'Where do you expect to go?' she asked as she followed him into the hall.

'Up over the top for a breath of Border air,' James smiled. 'I may even go as far as Sun Hill to see what Elliott thinks about leasing me some of his grazing land. He knows I'm interested.'

'Amy will like that,' Margot said, a forlorn wistfulness clouding her eyes. 'She's still very attached to Nellie, and thinks she should know about the pup from time to time. Meanwhile,' she added, 'I suppose I could take said pup to the village when I go to post my letters. He's used to the lead now, and not quite so hysterical when he sees the signs of ''walkies''!'

Her father came to the dining-room door.

'I'm off down to the river,' he announced, 'to take a look at that stretch of water above the falls. It looks good to me, and I dare say you could do with another fish for the pot.'

'Are you going alone?' Margot asked, wondering if he had made a rendezvous with Elliott when last they met.

'Absolutely! The fish don't appreciate conversation.' He grinned.

'Be careful,' she said automatically. 'Don't wade out too far. You'll remember about dinner, I hope. It's at eight o'clock!'

'Mrs Daley has made me a sandwich,' he said. 'She understands about fishermen!'

Margot watched them go their separate ways, her father to the riverbank with rod and net, James and his happy little daughter riding out together, side by side, with the sunlight dancing on Amy's curls and

the wind in their faces. It was such a change for
James, she acknowledged, riding out on to the high
moor with a fresh wind blowing against him instead
of a whirl of hot sand, and Amy, too, was in her
element, urging the pony on to keep up with the
mare which her father had reined in to a respectable
trot. It could always be like this, she thought, father
and daughter reconciled to each other, at last. She felt
sure that her brother would marry again eventually
and make his family complete.

'I'm going down to the post office,' she called to
Mrs Daley when she was ready to go out. 'I'll be back
in time to help you with lunch.'

Elspeth Daley followed her to the back door.

'Mr Kennedy was asking me if I could live in,' she
announced. 'I don't see much need for it, but he said
you might have to go to London occasionally and he
wasn't very good at looking after himself. There's the
wee one, too,' she added. 'He thought there should
be someone in the house all the time to look after her
properly.'

'Could we talk about it before I go to London?'
Margot suggested. 'I'd certainly like to feel there was
someone here all the time, Mrs Daley—someone like
yourself.'

Elspeth beamed.

'I wasn't very sure at first,' she admitted, 'but now
I've come to know you better, I feel I could arrange
things to live in for a while. The work isn't hard and I
could go down to the village to see to my family from
time to time.'

Returning from the village with an ecstatic pup still
tugging hopefully on the lead, Margot decided to let
him run free for a while. It was no more than eleven
o'clock and Mrs Daley wouldn't need her help in the
kitchen for some time yet.

She chose the path along the side of the bluebell wood, wondering how far James and his daughter had gone, but when she finally came to the boundary fence there was no sign of them anywhere on the moor. She walked on till she could see Sun Hill in the distance, but it seemed to be deserted, standing up there remotely with no sign of life around. The sheep were grazing farther down in the hollow of the hills and there was no sign of the collies anywhere.

A distant barking held her attention for a moment, making Duster prick up his ears expectantly, but finally it died away in the distance without a sight or sign of the collies or anyone else.

'Back home now!' she ordered, as Duster looked up at her with his red tongue hanging out. 'They must have gone another way.'

When she reached Ottershaws, however, Amy and her father had not returned.

'There's been no sign of them,' Elspeth Daley told her. 'They must have gone further than you expected.'

Margot glanced at her watch.

'They're generally back by this time. Anyway, I'll set the table, Mrs Daley.'

'It's all done,' Elspeth announced in that indulgent way she had when she was well-ahead with her work. 'Off you go and put your feet up for half an hour before they come back.'

'It seems strange that I didn't see them somewhere on their way home,' Margot said.

The telephone bell rang before Elspeth could reply, and Margot went to answer it. When she lifted the receiver her brother's voice came through, loud and clear. 'Margot, can you get over here?' he asked. 'There's been an accident.'

'Not—Amy?' She held her breath.

'Oh, no! I'm sorry,' he added quickly. 'Amy's all

right, if a bit shaken. It's Elliott.'

Her blood ran cold.

'Are you still there?' he asked.

'Yes—yes! What happened?'

The words had come in a whisper, while her heart-beats seemed to thunder aloud in the confined space of the alcove where the telephone stood.

'Clarinda bolted and upset the pony. We were coming down from Sun Hill and Elliott saw it all from the doorway,' James explained. 'He headed the pony off and got Amy out of the saddle, so I wasn't a lot of good to him, and then he was just lying there——'

Obviously agitated by what had occurred, he paused to draw breath.

'Is he—badly injured?' Margot whispered.

'We don't know. He was conscious and we've sent for the doctor, so he should be here any time now. I have to stay—there's nobody else—but I thought you'd better come and get Amy. She's a bit upset.'

'I'll come right away.' Suddenly her hands were trembling. 'I'll bring the car.'

All the way to Sun Hill by the main road through the village, the cry in her heart was 'Elliott!' She could not think of him crippled or injured in any way, but the fact was that James had told her so little. What was he holding back?

Sitting upright with her hands clamped hard on the steering-wheel, she drove through the village without actually noticing that she had done so, and soon she was on the steep ascent to the moor with Sun Hill up there on the hill ahead of her and a white ambulance already at the door. They were taking Elliott to Galashiels to the hospital!

When she finally drove up, he was being carried out on a stretcher.

Pulling out of the way and round the gable end of the house, she was just in time to see the ambulance doors being closed and the driver returning to the front seat.

'Please!' she cried, running forward, but nobody seemed to hear.

A great blackness came over her, as if the sun had suddenly disappeared behind a bank of gathering cloud, and then James was by her side and Amy, clinging to her hand.

'They're taking Elliott to the hospital,' her brother told her gently. 'The doctor wants to be quite sure about his leg, and there's further damage to his shoulder. He's going to be all right, Margot—I'm sure of it. He has tremendous strength.'

'Was he—unconscious when they took him away?' was all she could think of to ask, because Elliott's eyes had been closed.

'The doc gave him something for the pain,' James explained. 'Elliott protested, of course, but it was no good. Come and meet the doc.'

She took Amy's hand, leading her back into the house where the local doctor was busy repacking his medical bag.

'I always said horses were for pulling carts or walking behind a plough,' he observed, looking up as they went in. 'But now all that's a thing of the past we give them too little to do and sometimes they rebel. That mare of yours is far too finely bred, Kennedy, if you ask me. She looks as if she might have come from racing stock, and she'll take a lot of handling.'

'She was startled,' James defended his mount. 'Something—probably a young hare—darted out of the heather and the pony got in her way. It was an accident.'

'Hmm!' the doctor observed. 'Could have been worse, I suppose.' He looked down at Amy. 'And now, young lady, how about you? Are you all in one piece,' he asked, 'or do we need a bandage somewhere?'

Amy shook her head.

'Mr Dundass got me down before I was thrown,' she pointed out. 'It wasn't my pony's fault.'

'Of course it wasn't,' Margot agreed, thankful that Amy could talk about the accident so calmly, but still thinking about Elliott. 'What will happen now?' she asked.

The doctor looked about him.

'He'll want to come back here as soon as the hospital has stitched him up,' he said. 'I know Elliott. He's cussedly determined, and he thinks nobody can do the job but himself.'

'I'm quite willing to look after the sheep till he gets back,' James offered. 'Gavin and old Ned will give me a hand, so he needn't worry in that respect.'

'Who's going to tell him not to worry?' The doctor's eyes twinkled. 'Rather you than me,' he said.

'I'll have a word with him at the hospital,' James promised. 'I owe him.'

'The wee lass is all right.' The doctor ruffled Amy's curls. 'She did as she was told and no harm came to her, but I'd get her on that pony again as soon as you can, if I were you. Before she has time to think about what might have happened,' he added.

James looked at Margot.

'We'll have to get the horses back to Ottershaws,' she said. 'I'll never be able to trust Clarinda again.'

'She's as docile as a lamb now, tethered out there at the back beside the pony,' James pointed out. 'She had a fright and that was how it was. It could have happened to anyone.'

'But it happened to Elliott!' Margot protested, deeply shaken. 'And he has to work up here to earn a living.'

'We'll do all we can,' James promised. 'He may not be away too long.'

'We don't know that!' she said sharply, and then instantly, 'Oh, Jamie, I'm sorry! I didn't mean to bawl you out like that. It's just that—all this has been so sudden and it could have been so much worse. As it is,' she added swiftly, 'we don't know yet how badly Elliott is hurt—whether he will ever be able to work again.'

He put a comforting arm about her shoulders, seeing more than she realised.

'I feel I have to go to the hospital to find out,' he told her. 'If I take the car, could you walk Amy and the pony back to Ottershaws? I'll put Clarinda in the old sheep fold till I can pick her up later. She's calmed down now and she won't come to any further harm.'

'You'll phone as soon as you hear about Elliott?' she asked.

'I promise,' he said. 'But don't worry any more. Everything's going to be OK. Just tidy up a bit in here and close the door behind you.'

He was giving her something to do while she waited for news of Elliott, and she was grateful.

'Amy will help,' she said as he got into the car.

Sun Hill was untidy but clean enough, she discovered, thinking of Cathy for the first time. If she had been here, Cathy would have been the first one at the hospital or would even have insisted on going in the ambulance to be at Elliott's side, but Cathy had gone out with her advanced students and there was no way of contacting her, apart from phoning through to the Mains, which she would do once she had returned to Ottershaws.

Applying herself to the task of tidying up, she was glad of the physical effort which took part of her mind away from the agonising throught of Elliott's injuries. He had done it for Amy, she reflected,

did hold with galloping across the moor on the back of a horse, anyway. Something was sure to happen, sooner or later.'

Margot wasn't listening. All she wanted to hear was that Elliott was alive and would return to Sun Hill eventually.

'I don't want to phone the hospital,' she said. 'They'll be busy enough without me bothering them, and James will soon be home.'

'He said something about phoning Lowther Mains,' Elspeth mentioned. 'He wanted Cathy Graeme to know.'

'I'll get in touch with Cathy,' Margot offered. 'She's been away all day.'

'She'll be as anxious as you are, I dare say,' Elspeth decided, shaking her head. 'Elliott Dundass is a lucky man having so many people worrying about him!'

'We're neighbours,' Margot said without thinking.

Janet Graeme answered her call when she phoned Lowther Mains.

'I don't want to worry you, Mrs Graeme,' Margot began, 'but Elliott's had an accident and I thought Cathy——'

'Cathy already knows,' Janet said breathlessly, 'and she's away to the hospital. Your brother phoned her.'

'Oh!' Margot clutched the receiver. 'Is there any more news, Mrs Graeme?'

'Just that Elliott's leg has been put in plaster and his shoulder has been set.'

'His shoulder?'

'That was damaged, too. Dear me!' Janet sighed. 'It looks as if he will be out of circulation for quite a while, which could be a disaster as far as Sun Hill is concerned with the shearing and the dipping coming up, but you won't know much about that, will you, you not being used to the working of a farm?'

'I can guess how important it is, Mrs Graeme,' Margot acknowledged, 'and how unfortunate, but I'm sure my brother will do all he can to help.'

'We all will,' Janet agreed. 'Especially Cathy. As I've just said, she's off to the hospital to see what she can do in the meantime.'

'I must keep in touch,' Margot answered bleakly, feeling that she had been brushed aside.

When James drove back to Ottershaws, Cathy came with him, driving her own car.

'I came to see how Amy was,' she explained. 'She must have had quite a shock.'

'We're putting her to bed early,' Margot said, 'but I think she'll be all right by morning. Elliott made it easy for her.'

'And got himself into a packet of trouble!' was the prompt rejoinder. 'He'll be no use up there at Sun Hill for some time with a broken leg and his arm in a sling. I know it was an accident, but it needn't have happened to Elliott, of all people!'

'We're terribly sorry about it,' Margot said, excusing the rudeness. 'I know it needn't have happened, Cathy, but these things do, and now we must help Elliott all we can.'

Cathy looked at her shrewdly.

'What can you possibly do?' she echoed in her mother's measured tones. 'You don't know the first thing about farming. James might be able to help, though,' she decided, 'and he could learn a bit about sheep while he was at it.'

'I've offered,' James informed her, coming up to join them, 'but Elliott thinks he'll be back in harness in a day or two, and doesn't need help.'

'Preserve me from dogmatic men!' Cathy exclaimed. 'He's quite mad, of course. He'll be hobbling about on crutches for ages, even if his

shoulder does mend miraculously in the meantime.
It's a good thing I'm here to take charge,' she
concluded.

'Who better?' James grinned. 'You know most of
the answers.'

'I hope so,' Cathy agreed, confidently enough.
'And I know Sun Hill. I can arrange about the
shearing when the time comes, and the dipping too. I
won't let Elliott down.'

It seemed to Margot that Cathy had forgotten
about her in her plans for Sun Hill and the future,
forgotten about James, too, in her eagerness to help
an old friend. Perhaps that was how it should be,
she thought, although her heart was now as heavy as
lead.

'I'll take you over to Sun Hill to collect Clarinda,'
Cathy offered as James prepared to walk across the
moor. 'Do you really mean to sell her?'

'After today I won't have much confidence in her,'
James answered. 'I'm sorry, but I have to protect
Amy and I don't want her exposed to another
accident.'

'We'll buy Clarinda back from you,' Cathy offered.
'She'll make a good breeding mare once she's settled
down. Do you want to buy another horse?'

'A quiet one,' James stipulated.

Two days later Elliott came back to Sun Hill. In spite
of what Cathy had said, Margot had decided to
do what she could in the little house to prepare
for his homecoming, getting in stores, changing
bed-linen which she had washed at Ottershaws and
hung out to dry in the sharp, strong wind which
came down from the hills before she returned it
to make up the bed in the room he used at the back
of the house. Quite sure that he would be kept
at the hospital for at least a week, she took her

time, polishing and dusting till everything shone,
while the boy, Gavin, and old Ned looked after the
sheep.

Each day James had come from his visit to the
hospital to help them, and even though he was still
anxious about Elliott's condition he seemed to be in
his element.

'This is the life!' he declared. 'I feel I should go for
it now in a big way.'

Cathy came and went, ordering the men about,
but she still had her commitments at the riding-
school with a local gymkhana in the near future
to contend with and her pupils' high hopes to
consider.

'I can't be away all the time,' she explained, 'and
Elliott wouldn't think of it. He's fiercely independent, you know, and he doesn't like to feel
obliged.'

Especially to strangers, Margot thought, and to one
stranger in particular who seemed to have betrayed
his brother! Well, he must never know who had
tidied up at Sun Hill while he had been away, and no
doubt he would give all the credit to Cathy when he
came to think about it.

When the ambulance drew up at the front of the
house she was in the kitchen feeding the collies,
and she called out when the door opened, thinking
that it was her brother.

'I'm in here, Jamie! Have you been to the hospital?'

Since there was no immediate answer she went
quickly along the passage, fearing what she might
hear, but instead of her brother she came face to face
with one of the ambulance man, and saw Elliott
standing immediately behind him. His arm half-in
and half-out of a sling, he was leaning heavily on a
steel crutch, with the ambulance driver supporting
him on the other side.

'Here he is, ma'am,' the driver informed her. 'He just wouldn't stay in another day. Said he had to get back to work and signed himself out in spite of everybody telling him to have patience and wait till he was properly fit.'

Elliott stood quite still, looking at her with the level stare which had once disconcerted her so much.

'What are you doing here?' he asked.

'Seeing that you come home to a clean bed and a tidy house.' Her lips felt parched as the words rushed out. 'I didn't expect you home so soon.'

The ambulance men prepared to leave.

'You'll be all right now, Mr Dundass,' the driver said. 'You won't be needing us any more. The doctor will be in to see you before long, so in the meantime be good!'

Elliott was still looking at Margot as they closed the door and drove off down the hill road in second gear till they reached the bridge across the river and turned on to the main road.

'I could have managed,' he said stiltedly, 'but thank you all the same. I know you feel obliged, but there's no reason to.'

She caught her breath.

'We *are* obliged, Elliott, if that's the word we have to use,' she said firmly. 'We can't get away from the fact that you probably saved Amy's life, and we'll be eternally grateful no matter how much you try to deny it.'

'It was an emergency and I suppose I acted promptly,' he agreed, 'but that was all there was to it—a quick reaction which saved a calamity.' He glanced about him at the tidy living-room with its highly polished grate and sparkling window-panes. 'There was no need for you to do all this.'

They stood looking at each other, undecided what to say next.

'Let me make you a cup of tea,' Margot offered.

She wanted to take him in her arms, to comfort him and press his head close against her breast, but how could she do that when he was determined to stand aloof, scorning all help except, perhaps, from James, who had become his friend?

Gently she led him to the armchair in the corner beside the fireplace, laying his crutch close to hand.

'I'll light the fire,' she offered. 'You must feel cold.'

'I feel shattered,' he answered, 'finding you here like this. It makes nonsense of my former attitude, you see, like rubbing salt into an open wound.'

She found the other crutch, placing it beside the chair.

'Don't let us discuss it again, Elliott,' she begged. 'Let's just say I was trying to be neighbourly, although I know you don't want that, but what could I do when you put us so firmly in your debt?'

It wasn't what she had meant to say, but it had to suffice because she was so utterly shaken by his unexpected return.

'I could do with that cup of tea,' he said.

She went to the kitchen, standing for a moment against the sink before she filled the kettle, her eyes misted by sudden pain. It was so small a task, yet it might be the last one she would ever do for him.

When she carried in the tray with two cups and saucers on it, he took it for granted that she would join him.

'What did they say at the hospital?' she asked, pouring the milk she had brought with her into each cup in turn. 'They were probably angry when you decided to return here.'

The remark made him smile.

'They were never really angry,' he said. 'They just thought me unwise.'

'You were, you know.' She passed him his cup. 'You should have stayed there at least till your shoulder recovered. No doubt they thought you stubborn and uncooperative, to say the least.'

'Which is true enough,' he mused. 'I don't like being fenced in, which is about my only excuse.'

'You can't manage here on your own,' she pointed out, passing him the biscuit tin she had filled for his return. 'Who is going to cook for you?'

'I have one good arm,' he assured her, 'and soon it will be two.'

'Not if you don't take care,' she declared. 'Cathy said you were stubborn, and I think she was right.'

'Margot,' he bent forward to look at her, 'don't worry about me. Long ago I learned how to fend for myself, and it's no different now.'

'You weren't handicapped then!' she objected. 'You could get about as much as you wanted, but now you have to rely on two elbow-crutches to see you through. It's not—civilised,' she added flatly.

'Would it be more civilised if you were allowed to wheel me around in a bath-chair?' he asked. 'Utterly dependent?'

'It would make a lot more sense!' she told him hotly. 'You don't want to appear dependent—we know that—but James and I can't just stand aside when we feel so desperately grateful.'

His penetrating blue eyes searched her face.

'I know all about your gratitude,' he said. 'James has made it very clear, but give me credit for doing it for Amy too. I couldn't just stand by and see her injured, could I?'

'No. But please don't try to belittle the fact that you probably saved her life. And please let us offer our help,' she added quietly.

He put his cup down on the saucer, pushing it away from him.

'I've already accepted James's help,' he told her. 'It's a sort of mutual thing—his physical strength against my know-how. He wants to learn about sheep and this is his big opportunity. He'll help me to run Sun Hill for the time being until I'm on my feet again, and then we're going to talk about grazing. I've got more land than I need, and eventually he can run his own flock till he finds a larger place nearby.'

'Which won't be easy,' she said, picking up the tray. 'Thank you for considering James. He won't let you down, I can assure you.'

They had made all these decisions without her, she thought, but that was the way of things. Turning towards the door, she looked back at him where he sat in the chair beside the fire with his eyes closed.

'I think you ought to go to bed,' she said.

Instantly the blue eyes opened to regard her coldly.

'I can do that for myself,' he assured her. 'I may be on crutches for the moment, but I'm not an invalid.'

'I'm sorry,' she said. 'I was only trying to be helpful.'

'I know that,' he agreed, 'but it isn't necessary. Thank you for all you have done, but—don't come back.'

When she reached the kitchen her hands were shaking. This was finality. He didn't want her at Sun Hill ever again.

When she was ready to go, she went to stand at the sitting-room door, looking towards the fire where he was sitting with his head bowed, his mouth hard and relentless as she had seen it many times before.

'I have to say goodbye,' she told him. 'I'll be going to London soon and—and I don't know when I'll be back.'

Suddenly his eyes were raised to hers.

'James told me,' he said. 'You're hoping you can continue your career, and I wish you the best of luck.'

'Oh, Elliott,' she said, 'I'm going to need it so much if I'm ever going to be happy again!'

When she got back to Ottershaws she had already come to her decision.

'I have to go to London next week,' she told her father as James came to the dining-room door. 'I'll arrange for Mrs Daley to sleep in while I'm away, and I'll phone you as soon as I have a definite decision about my voice.'

'But why now?' James objected. 'Why right away?'

'Because I have to adjust my life, to make plans for the future,' she tried to explain. 'We're all doing that in one way or another,' she pointed out. 'Elliott told me this afternoon that you intend to graze some of your own sheep on his land till you can find a place of your own, James, and I'm glad about that, but don't forget that you will be welcome here at Ottershaws for as long as you care to stay. If you would like to make it your permanent home, I have no wish to refuse you.'

Her father looked uncomfortable.

'What about you?' he asked. 'This was to have been your home for the next three years, at least.'

'I may have to make other plans,' she said huskily. 'About settling down nearer London if I'm able to go on with my career.' She drew a deep breath. 'It might even entail going to America for a year. Who knows?'

'I wish you sounded more enthusiastic about it,' James put in bluntly. 'I know you must be anxious about your interview with the voice man in Harley Street, or wherever, but it must be a foregone conclusion. Your voice sounds perfect to me.'

'Margot can't be the judge of that,' Andrew Kennedy declared. 'She must take the professional advice she has asked for and act accordingly. Have you heard from Henry Levitt?' he asked, turning to his daughter again. 'He has done a lot for you in the past.'

'Dear Henry!' Margot smiled. 'He's had such a lot to contend with, it's a wonder he bothers with me at all.'

'He's got faith in you,' Andrew said, sitting down at the head of the table. 'So have we all. I must confess I'd like to see you get to the top one of these days. It's a pardonable sin to take pride in one's offspring, I suppose, and I'll keep hoping for your future success. At the same time, I'm selfish enough to want to see more of you, so I hope you'll be coming back to Ottershaws quite often.'

She could hardly bear their concern for her, the tears choking in her throat.

'It might not be easy,' she said, 'but I won't go off anywhere without contacting you first, I promise.'

She knew that her ultimate happiness mattered to them, and that was a comfort, although it didn't make her parting with Ottershaws any easier.

In the morning James went off with Cathy and her father to buy some sheep at a neighbouring farm, and she was left to wonder about Elliott's plight at Sun Hill without Cathy's help. She could not go there, however, after being rejected by Elliott so completely, and Cathy would no doubt go up with James when he took his new flock to Sun Hill later in the day.

She saw them up there on the side of the hill towards four o'clock, the two men running the sheep into the fold at the side of the house while Elliott looked on. They were too far away to be seen in any detail, but she had the decided impression that they would work well together through a mutual interest.

When James returned, he was full of enthusiasm for his new way of life.

'As soon as we can get them marked with my own brand we can put the sheep out on to the hill,' he explained. 'I'll graze the far side of the moor and down into Turrufdale for a start, and that way we can share the shearing and the dipping when the time comes. I quite fancy my hand at the shearing,' he grinned, 'although I don't suppose I'll be any use at it for a year or two. That's Cathy's opinion, anyway!'

He was talking in terms of the distant future, and she was glad for Amy's sake, at least.

As for her own future, it was bound by the vaguest uncertainty, and all she could do was to follow that inconstant star.

She did not see Elliott again, not even at a distance.

CHAPTER SEVEN

THEY went as a family in the early morning to see her
off on the Edinburgh to London train. The platform at
Berwick was high and cold, with a haar seeping in
from the North Sea to shroud the view across the
Tweed in a pale mist, like a country of the heart
veiled in tears.

'When will you come back?' Amy wanted to know,
slipping a small, cold hand into Margot's as they said
goodbye. 'Tomorrow?'

'Perhaps—one day after that,' Margot said, not
wanting to lie. 'You'll be good while I'm away?'

Amy nodded, taking her father's hand.

When the train drew out they were standing in line
on the deserted platform, waving until she couldn't
see them any more. Something final seemed to be
happening, something which would inevitably draw
them further and further apart.

When she reached King's Cross a fine rain was
falling, and because there was no one there to meet
her she took a taxi from the station rank to the hotel
where she had booked in for a week until she could
make other, more permanent arrangements. Gazing
out on the grey pavements, with the hurrying
multitude huddled under umbrellas, it all looked so
desolate, but that might be because she was
contrasting it with the wide, open greenness of the
fells and the lush Border country she had left behind
her so reluctantly.

The hotel she had chosen was central to her
requirements since her first appointment would be
with the Harley Street specialist who had told her to

rest her voice for a while before she attempted to sing again. It was also within walking distance of Henry Levitt's office, where he also maintained a small, one-bedroomed flat. Henry, she had always felt, was the eternal bachelor, although he was kind, considerate and very distinguished-looking, giving the lie to the usual conception of a successful theatrical agent.

For the first time she realised how much she had missed him, his work and humour and his unfailing interest in her career. She would phone him as soon as possible to arrange a meeting.

The hotel was small and full of guests at that time of year; people on holiday, people shopping, people meeting each other in the busy foyer, shaking hands and kissing, glad to be together again after a parting, perhaps. There was laughter everywhere and the buzz of eager conversation.

Feeling desperately alone, she turned to the lift where a porter was waiting with her luggage.

'Your first visit, madam?'

'Oh, no! I used to live in London. I may come back to live here again. I haven't seen you in the hotel before.'

'No, madam. I'm new. Just got the job, as a matter of fact, and glad to have it. I've always wanted to work in London.'

They had reached the third floor.

'Where do you come from?' Margot asked absently.

'Aberdyfi. That's in Wales, madam. There was nothing much there for me, so I took a chance. London's the real place to be if you want to get to the top.'

The lift doors opened and Margot got out. Was that what she wanted now—to get to the top, to make a success of her chosen career which would fill in all the blank places in her heart and allow her to forget the past and all the pain of loving?

Coldly impersonal, the hotel corridor stretched before her with its row of numbered doors.

'Three-O-five,' the porter said, stepping back when he had opened the door. 'It's a nice room, madam—facing front.'

It would be no different from a hundred other hotel rooms, Margot thought, with its adjacent bathroom and spotless towels ready for her immediate use, and the fitted wardrobes and single, comfortable bed along the wall covered to match the curtains at the window. Then, suddenly, it was different. A magnificent bouquet of flowers lay waiting for her on the dressing-table, a welcoming tribute which had surely come from Henry.

'Thank you!' She turned to where the porter was stacking her luggage on the folding stool. 'Do you think you could find me a vase to put my flowers in?' she asked.

When he came back with the container, she was standing where he had left her with the small envelope which had come with the flowers still in her hand.

'Thank you!' she said again, but it was more to Henry Levitt than the young man who had come from Aberdyfi in Wales to take London by storm.

The card in the envelope said simply, 'Welcome back! With love from Henry.' For a long time she looked down at it, so many emotions churning in her heart that she could not attempt to sort them out, and then she arranged the mixed bouquet in the tall white vase and began to unpack, turning back to the flowers from time to time to reassure herself. Welcome back to London, with love from Henry!

Before she had washed and changed, the telephone rang and she rushed to answer it. Could it be from Ottershaws so soon after her arrival? Sitting down on the bed, she lifted the receiver.

'Henry!' she said, trying to keep the disappointment out of her voice. 'I was going to ring you to thank you for my beautiful flowers.'

She smiled when he said he hoped they hadn't been delivered the day before.

'I was out of town,' he explained. 'As a matter of fact, I've just got back. I was down at the cottage for the weekend, seeing about some repairs, but they're in hand now so I haven't got to worry so much.'

'I can't imagine anything ever worrying you,' she told him, 'unless it was an unfulfilled contract.'

'I've had some of those in my time, as you can guess. But enough of me. How are you, and what brings you back to London for so long a stay?'

'The voice,' she said, reminding him of her Harley Street appointment. 'It seems to be much better, Henry, but I can't be certain till I've seen Mr Carlton again.'

'When will that be?'

'Tomorrow.'

'So soon?' There was a slight pause while he made a calculation. 'We must meet this evening, in that case,' he decided. 'Can I pick you up at eight o'clock?'

'If you really aren't doing anything else,' she conceded.

'Nothing that won't cancel,' he assured her. 'Looking forward to it!'

He rang off abruptly, a busy man with a dozen other things to do.

She considered her wardrobe, selecting a midnight-blue cocktail dress which she had never worn at Ottershaws. It had been a different sort of life there, she mused, tweeds and warm dresses chosen more for their practicality than for glamour, and she had never felt the need for her London wardrobe until now. Henry would choose a discreet little restaurant

somewhere in the West End, but it would be full of
people bent on enjoying themselves and she couldn't
let him down.

Before she ran her bath she phoned Ottershaws,
holding her breath as the call went through.

'Ottershaws.' James's voice came clearly over the
line.

'Hello, I'm here! I thought I'd better phone you
before I went out,' she explained, 'just to let you
know I've arrived all in one piece.'

'And making the most of your visit right away,' her
brother suggested. 'Where are you off to tonight?'

'Oh—just out with Henry,' she answered. 'I
suppose it's what one might call a business meeting.
Jamie, how is everyone—Amy and Dad and Mrs
Daley?'

'Much as you left them this morning!' His tone was
amusedly dry.

'Yes, I suppose it is foolish of me to ask,' she
allowed, 'but it does seem such an age since we
parted and London is so grim. It's raining,' she
added, 'and everybody is in such a hurry!'

'You know the answer to that,' he said. 'Come back
here with the next train!'

'I can't do that. I have to see Mr Carlton in the
morning.'

'You know what his answer will be. You're fine!'

'I hope that will be his verdict. Has Amy been out
with Cathy this afternoon?'

'As a matter of fact, Cathy's here now,' James told
her. 'We've persuaded her to stay for something to
eat with us.'

'Oh—that's nice, but what about Elliott?' she added
breathlessly.

'He appears to be managing quite well. I was up
there this afternoon talking sheep with him for a
couple of hours, and he seems to be reconciled to the

crutches now. I suppose you can become used to anything after a while, especially if your bread and butter depends on it,' he mused.

'Surely you can keep him from doing too much till his shoulder improves, at least?' she suggested. 'I know what Elliott's like.'

'I wonder if you do,' he said eloquently. 'He's not half so arrogant as you think. When are you coming back?'

'I don't know, Jamie.' Her fingers fastened tightly over the receiver. 'I have so many decisions to make.'

'Well—you know what we feel if you want to come!'

When he rang off she sat looking at the instrument for a full minute before her lips moved.

'Oh, I want to come,' she said. 'I want to come so much, but how can I ever do that while Elliott thinks of me as he does?'

Henry was waiting for her in the hall when she went down, elegant, as always, in an immaculately tailored suit and silk shirt, his hair streaked at the temples with white, which only served to make him look more distinguished than ever.

'Margot!' he cried, holding out his arms. 'How lovely to see you!' He kissed her on both cheeks, a habit she had almost forgotten. 'My car's outside. Did you have a good journey from Berwick?'

'Very pleasant.' She put her hand on his arm. 'It was very fast and, anyway, I wanted to leave the car for my family to use.'

'That family of yours!' he said, leading her to the door. 'You give them too much thought. What has happened to your brother, by the way? You said he had gone up there to see you.'

'James is still there.' They got into the Porsche standing at the kerb. 'He's talking about staying there—settling down in Britain for good.'

'High time!' he observed, starting the engine.
'You've been *in loco parentis* long enough.'

They joined the stream of traffic heading west.

'It will take a lot of the responsibility for Amy off
your shoulders,' he added candidly, 'and I can't
pretend to be sorry about that. You've been a
wonderful surrogate mother to that child, but now
it's time to think about yourself and what *you* want to
do.'

'I won't be able to make any decision before I've
seen Mr Carlton,' Margot reminded him.

'Of course not,' he agreed, steering the car into the
park. 'I can almost tell you his verdict, though. You
sound very good to me.'

'I hope that's true,' she said. 'I hope I won't have
to go back to see him again.'

They reached the restaurant he had chosen off
Princes Gate, where a table had been reserved for
them in a secluded corner.

'We have a lot to talk about,' he said, 'so I chose a
quiet spot.'

The sounds and the lights of London seemed to be
pressing in on her even in this quiet place, but she
had chosen to come back here—perhaps for good.

'No matter what happens tomorrow, Henry,' she
warned him, 'I won't be able to take up an
appointment immediately. I suppose you know that
I'll have to have further tuition to make sure of my
voice.'

'Back to square one, do you mean?' he asked.

'Almost.'

He looked disappointed as he ordered their drinks.

'I thought we might have managed New York
again,' he said, 'but I see what you mean. You
wouldn't be giving yourself a fair chance in the
circumstances.'

'Give me till the autumn,' she said slowly. 'That

should be time enough.'

'I'll work on it,' he assured her as the waiter handed her a menu. 'And now tell me all you've been doing up there in the wilds of Scotland.'

'It isn't wild at all,' she protested. 'Just very, very beautiful.'

He regarded her curiously while she ran her eyes down the menu.

'Is that all it had to offer?' he asked.

A hot colour stained her cheeks.

'Not all,' she said, 'but—the other things have ceased to count.'

'Such as?' he asked.

She hesitated.

'Like making a home and friends, and learning to live without all the trimmings.'

He looked about him at the 'trimmings' she had so easily discarded.

'You could never have lived in a backwater without regret,' he told her decidedly. 'You have a great talent and you must use it.'

'Please, could we talk about something else?' she begged. 'I can't promise you anything, Henry. Not yet.'

They spoke of mutual friends and what he had been doing while she had been away.

'Henry,' she asked, 'do you remember someone called Nigel Grantley?'

He considered her question as he finished his soup.

'Should I?' he asked. 'I meet so many people, and not all of them interesting.'

'He was quite young and he came from Scotland.'

'With a name like that, where else?'

'His real name was Neil Dundass.' She gazed down at her empty plate. 'I've met his family,' she added unsteadily. 'At least, I've met his elder brother. As a matter of fact, I rented Ottershaws from him.'

'Something of a coincidence,' he suggested as the waiter moved away. 'They happen all the time.'

'I don't think it was quite that.' She was determined to speak about Neil, to get him out of her system, perhaps. 'He was always talking about Scotland—about where he lived—as if it was the perfect place, and I think that influenced me in my choice when I decided to go to the Borders to find a home.'

'Now I know who you mean,' Henry said, looking down at the excellent steak which had been placed before him. 'Tall, rangy sort of chap with piercing eyes. Thought he was a second Noel Coward or something like that. A bit of a nuisance, I thought, hanging about the way he did when he hadn't any real talent to show for it.'

'He was desperately ambitious,' Margot pointed out.

'Aren't they all? What happened to him?'

'He was killed in an accident—driving a sports car too fast.'

'How well did you know him?' he asked after a pause.

She drew a swift breath.

'That's just the point, Henry. I didn't know him at all apart from reading one or two of his plays and trying to give him some advice.'

'Out of sympathy, I expect.' He smiled across the table at her.

'I was sorry for him—yes.'

He continued to look at her with a measure of doubt in his eyes.

'You're not letting this worry you?' He touched her hand. 'You weren't in the least responsible. It's not as if you just brushed him off without a thought when he pestered you so much. You read his dreadful plays.'

'He imagined himself in love with me.'

'You couldn't have done anything about that,' he decided. 'Some of these young would-be writers develop the most amazing fantasies, generally about successful people. They come to London expecting so much, hoping to write immortal prose and be recognised immediately, and then, when it doesn't happen, they go to pieces, sometimes in a spectacular way. They see success all around them, but never manage to achieve it, so they cotton on to someone else's fame. It's a sort of second-hand experience that could never really satisfy them. The Americans call it ''celebrity-stalking''—an unkind description which explains a lot—and in his case it probably became an obsession. He recognised your success and the possible glamour of your future, and so he hung around, hoping some of it might brush off on him one day.'

'He hung around wherever I went until it became embarrassing,' Margot confessed, 'yet, curiously enough, he never actually spoke of love to me. That was the hidden part—the fantasy, if you like. He had to prove success to himself, I think, convincing himself that I loved him when I hardly knew him at all. He was a few years my junior, and I could never have married him even if he had asked me. Instead——' She moistened her lips that had suddenly gone dry. 'Instead he wrote it all down in a diary which his brother found.'

'This brother of his,' Henry asked after a moment's thought. 'What is he like?'

'Older than Neil was, and very proud of his family ties.'

'Yet he let you rent Ottershaws?'

'He didn't know who I was when we first met. It was one of your coincidences, Henry!'

'But he knows now?'

'Yes, I'm afraid so.'

'Will you go back to Scotland?' he asked.

'I—don't think so. Henry, I don't really know what I shall do,' she said.

'First things first,' he advised. 'See what happens tomorrow and then phone me.'

She took his advice, walking from the hotel to Harley Street where her appointment was for eleven o'clock. Sitting alone in the panelled waiting-room with the heavy door closed behind her, she felt desperately alone and yet she had comfort of a sort in Henry. Last night he had done everything he could to cheer her up, dismissing their conversation about Ottershaws because he had seen how much it had distressed her, to talk about the busy international world of music instead. At least he has faith in me, she thought. Dear Henry, who knew her so well! He had never married, dedicating himself to his work, and his had been a success story too, but once he had told her of a love he had cherished long ago, a childhood sweetheart he had never forgotten. 'She married someone else,' he had said, 'and I came back to London and married my job. A sad little story, I'm afraid!'

When the door opened, she followed the doctor's receptionist to his consulting-room on the first floor, nervous now that she was to hear his final verdict so soon.

He talked all the time to give her confidence, making his examination thoroughly before he sat back in his chair with an encouraging smile.

'The Border air must have worked wonders,' he decided. 'You're as good as new, but that doesn't mean you can sing your heart out immediately,' he went on to warn her. 'Take things one step at a time and give your voice a chance. Go back to Scotland

and relax for a while.'

'I don't think I can do that,' she found herself saying. 'Sooner or later I'll have to go back to work. I thought—a few singing lessons wouldn't come amiss.'

'By all means,' he agreed. 'Don't overdo it and you'll be ready for grand opera before the end of the year!'

She smiled at his little joke.

'I feel so relieved,' she confessed. 'Thank you, Mr Carlton, for all your help.'

'It was a pleasure.' He put a fatherly arm about her shoulders as she rose to go. 'Next thing, we'll be seeing your name in lights, as the saying is!'

She smiled at that too as they said goodbye.

She was free! The awful burden of uncertainty about her voice had been lifted from her shoulders by a few kind words, and she was grateful. She phoned Ottershaws immediately.

'It's me!' she said when Amy answered the phone. 'Where's everybody?'

'In the garden. Cathy's there, too,' Amy volunteered, adding excitedly, 'I'm going to be a bridesmaid!'

'A bridesmaid?' Margot repeated. 'Whatever made you think of that?'

'Cathy said I could be one when she gets married.' The thin, proud voice came across the line quite clearly. 'That will be nice, won't it, Aunty Margot?'

'Very nice, darling!' Margot couldn't ask when Cathy expected to be married or to whom. 'Can you get Grandpa for me?'

'Yes, I'll go and tell him.'

While she waited she could only think about Elliott—Elliott and Cathy planning to marry now that Cathy was so desperately needed at Sun Hill!

'Hello!' her father called. 'What news?'

'I appear to be one hundred per cent fit.'

'Does that mean you'll be coming home?'

She hesitated.

'Not yet.' She was still thinking about Elliott. 'I have to have singing-lessons again to break in my voice gradually, I suppose, but it shouldn't take long.'

'No doubt the lessons will have to be in London,' he suggested with a note of disappointment in his deep voice. 'Edinburgh wouldn't be a possibility?'

'It would be best to go back to Miss Steiger, Dad.'

'Yes, I suppose so. Edinburgh was just a passing thought.'

'Have you—any other news?' she asked.

'About Elliott, do you mean? He's fine. As a matter of fact he was out on the moor today with Jamie and they've come to a final arrangement about the grazing. I think Jamie's been a tremendous help to him when he can't get around so well and he appreciates it. He's managing all right on the crutches but they're a bit restricting, as you can imagine. He feels frustrated and that makes him angry.'

'I can understand that,' Margot agreed. 'And how is Cathy?'

'She's here now.' He paused for a moment. 'She's very fond of that enterprising granddaughter of mine,' he laughed. 'Amy seems to be able to twist Cathy round her little finger!'

'They hit it off practically from the start,' Margot said flatly. 'At first I thought it wasn't going to work, and then—suddenly they were friends.'

'It's often the way,' Andrew Kennedy agreed. 'Will we see you soon?'

'One day,' she promised, 'but I really must go back to work now, even if it's only a few singing lessons to make sure I'm in the right key!'

'I'll give your love to the others,' he offered. 'Keep in touch!'

When he rang off, Margot stood with the dead receiver in her hand, wondering why he hadn't mentioned Cathy's intentions or the fact that Amy was to be bridesmaid. Perhaps nothing was settled yet, she thought, no definite date for Cathy's wedding.

She phoned Henry in the afternoon.

'What now?' he asked when he had heard her good news.

'Some extra singing lessons just to make sure the cure is complete,' she told him. 'I can't take the risk of damaging my voice by singing professionally without them. They'll be a warm-up for the future.'

'Do I hear a note of uncertainty in your voice?' he asked. 'You're not about to change your mind and go running back to Scotland?'

'That won't happen,' she said wistfully.

When she saw him again she had been in London for three weeks, and during this time she had contacted her old tutor and re-established herself in Miss Steiger's lofty studio overlooking the Thames.

'How's it all going?' Henry asked, meeting her for lunch.

'Like a house on fire, I suppose! I don't feel any strain at all, but Adele thinks I should have a holiday before I return to work in earnest.'

'Where would you go?' he asked, leading her to the table which had been reserved for them. 'Scotland?'

She shook her head.

'Somewhere nearer London,' she decided.

'Tell you what,' he suggested eagerly, 'why don't you go down to the cottage for a few days? It's habitable now, although a few workmen are still around. Nothing to worry you, though,' he added, seeing her hesitation. 'It's mostly in the attic. You'd be doing me a favour,' he added, 'when I can't get down there as often as I would like.'

'In that case,' she said, 'I'll go. Thank you, Henry, for being so—accommodating.'

'I'm being practical,' he pointed out.

'And you will tell me if I overstay my welcome?'

'It won't be for some time,' he assured her. 'I'm off to New York tomorrow.'

'You fly across the Atlantic as regularly as Concorde!'

'And half as cheaply! But I will fly Concorde when you make a spectacular living for us both in the near future!'

'Flatterer!' She kissed his cheek. 'You know I'm not that good.'

'Wait and see!' He applied himself to his platter of oysters. 'Why don't you have some of these? They're good for you.'

'I hear they have a devastating effect!' she laughed.

'Not on me,' he said. 'I just like them.'

Henry always made her laugh, and quite apart from that he was good for her morale.

When she had phoned Ottershaws again to acquaint them of her intentions, she prepared to leave London for Henry's cottage in Somerset. Nothing had been said about Cathy and Elliott's intentions, and she hadn't the courage to ask. After all, it took courage to hold out your heart to be finally broken by someone else's decision. She had asked as casually as she could how Elliott was, to be told that he was managing fine and the plaster would be off his leg by the end of the week. His shoulder, too, seemed to have mended. Otherwise, there was very little news, her father had assured her. Everything was just the same.

The longing in her was intense. If only she could go back just for a while to see them all, to stand on the open moor and smell the scent of heather and feel the keen wind on her face as she looked up to Sun Hill!

She went by train and hired a taxi from the station to take her to the cottage, which was more isolated than she had thought. It stood at the end of a narrow lane with a high beech hedge sheltering it, and it was everything Henry had described. Low eaves crouched over diamond-paned windows, and a magnificent magnolia spread its branches along the entire front wall, shedding creamy-white petals at her feet as she walked up the path to the front door. The cottage was over a hundred years old and had been greatly in need of repair when Henry had bought it, but he had restored it lovingly and the established garden which surrounded it would afford her much joy.

In some ways it reminded her of Ottershaws, although the two houses were entirely different.

Turning the key in the lock, she carried her suitcase inside to be instantly enchanted by the main room which was entered directly from the front door. Low wooden beams supported the ceiling which had been painted white like the walls, and Henry had chosen patterned chair covers in white and blue to match the white skin rugs on the polished wood floor—large white daisies on a background as blue as a cloudless summer sky.

It was a place for relaxation, and Henry had offered it to her for just that purpose.

After she had been there for a week she began to feel more relaxed. The village was half a mile away and she walked there each day to collect milk and newspapers, wondering on the way back if she should perhaps hire a bicycle, but she never did.

When she phoned Ottershaws, she was always assured that they were managing very well and that Cathy and the ponies were thriving, but there was no further news of Cathy's wedding. I'm too cowardly to ask the direct question, she thought, too sure that my heart would be broken by just one word.

A postcard arrived from Henry from New York to say that he would be returning to London before the end of the month. 'Mission accomplished,' he had added, which made her wonder what he had been up to. Perhaps he was trying to force her to a decision to make up her mind quite definitely about the future.

When there was no further communication from him for another week, she came to the conclusion that it wasn't particularly urgent, turning her attention back to the garden which had given her so much pleasure. She was gathering roses to fill the blue bowl in the living-room when she heard the sound of a car coming along the lane. It was travelling in second gear, finding its way carefully until it stopped at the wicket gate in the beech hedge. It was Henry's car.

Panic-stricken because she had been thinking about her final decision all morning without coming to any definite conclusion, she fled back into the house, laying the gathered roses on the table beside the bowl. What was she going to say to him? She knew the decision he wanted from her, she had known it all along and it would be almost disloyal of her to refuse.

He was a long time coming up the path, looking for her in the garden, perhaps, but she had left the door open and soon a man's tall figure was blocking it, a man far taller than Henry, and one who walked with the aid of a stick.

'Elliott!' She took a halting step towards him. 'Why have you come?' she asked huskily. 'Is it to accuse me again or—or is there bad news from Ottershaws?'

'Neither,' he said grimly. 'Can I come in?'

'Of course!' She stood aside to let him pass, her heart beating so strongly that he must have heard it. 'Please sit down. I thought it was Henry.'

He seemed to fill up the whole room, this love of

SHADOW ON THE HILLS

hers who would dominate her life forever.

'It is Henry's car,' he said evenly. 'He insisted I should borrow it when he saw that I couldn't walk very far. A very generous man, this Henry,' he observed, watching her as she lifted the roses to put them into the bowl.

'You've come a long way,' she said. 'Why?'

He moved then, coming to stand beside her at the table.

'I've come to ask your forgiveness,' he said, 'and to take you back to Ottershaws—if you will come.'

She couldn't answer him, unable to grasp the full meaning of his words, but their eyes met and suddenly she was in no doubt about the future.

'I love you,' he said. 'I should have told you that long ago. I've loved you since the moment I first saw you, Margot, there in my old home. I know you may never be able to forgive me for all I have said and done to you, but I do ask you to try. If we are to be neighbours up there in Scotland, we ought to live peaceably together.'

'Neighbours!' she cried. 'How can that be all when you have just said you love me? Oh, Elliott, all I want, all I'll ever want is to hear you say that again!'

Instantly she was in his arms, his lips on hers kissing her tenderly and then passionately, holding her as if he would never let her go, in a long moment of complete ecstasy which she wanted to go on forever. The scent of lavender wafting in through the open window was all about them, but she could think only of the scent of myrtle and heather blown on the wind across a high moor, with clouds scudding over it to brush away indecision and doubt.

Still in his arms, she told him about the decision she had to make before she saw Henry again.

'I promised myself I would give him his answer about my career when he returned from America,'

she said, 'and I thought he had come for it earlier
than I expected when I saw his car at the gate.'

'Is that why you ran away?' he asked in the
demanding tone she remembered so well, although
now there was a tenderness in it she could never have
dreamed of. 'Back into the house with all these roses in
your arms? It was like the day I saw you at Ottershaws,
only then it was daffodils you had picked.'

'I don't think I was running away, because I knew
that I couldn't promise Henry my future, after all,'
she confessed.

His arms tightened about her.

'Ah—Henry!' he returned as he kissed the blown
hair on her forehead. 'A most generous man, indeed!
He could have turned me away empty-handed when
I went to see him to ask for your address. I knew how
he felt about your career, and I was going to put paid
to his ambitions for you and all he did was lend me
his car to get here!' He held her more closely. 'I
thought I had lost you forever when Henry told me
how unjustly I had accused you, but I think I knew
that even before he told me the truth about Neil.'

He looked beyond her through the window,
remembering.

'I had cared for him so often,' he said. 'Helping
him out of scrapes, speaking up for him when he was
accused, blinding myself to his faults, maybe, but
Neil was Ottershaws to me and we were bound
together for better or for worse. I came to London to
tell you that, and I realise now that you wouldn't
break my faith in him because you knew me too
well.' His voice was suddenly harsh. 'I know that
never for one moment were you in love with him,
because you had recognised him for the impetuous
boy he was. Then, when he realised that the world
wasn't going to fall at his feet, that his work was
mediocre, he couldn't take it. Henry says that the

plays he submitted were erratic, without form and too hastily completed for him ever to succeed, but Neil wouldn't accept advice, which was something I already knew. He considered them masterpieces and developed a persecution complex, and very soon he was running wild, not even caring about success any more. When he died, it was the result of a horrendous accident. His car hit a tree and that was it.'

They stood remembering for a. moment, remembering the brother he had loved.

'It was left to Henry to tell me all this,' Elliott said at last, 'but now I know why you wouldn't even defend yourself.'

Margot put her arms about him.

'It's all over now,' she said, realising how hard it had been for him to talk so openly about Neil. 'I know you'll never forget him and I wouldn't want you to do that, but we have the future, Elliott—our future together.'

'I haven't a lot to offer you,' he protested. 'Just Sun Hill and a lot of hard work till we can get Ottershaws back.'

'I'm willing to chance that,' she told him, stretching up to kiss him on the cheek. 'It won't take long, Elliott, when we're doing it together. Let me get you something to eat,' she added, drawing herself reluctantly from the shelter of his arms. 'I'm sure you must be famished, as Cathy used to say!'

'How prosaic can you get?' He swept her off her feet in an effort to prove how much he had recovered from his accident. 'I love you for that, too,' he declared. 'You care for people, Margot. It never fails.'

While she grilled bacon in Henry's tiny kitchen he stood watching her, tall and windblown still, as she had first seen him.

'You haven't told me all I want to know about Ottershaws,' she accused him. 'How is everybody?'

'Anxious to have you back.' He put an arm about
her waist, drawing her to him as they watched the
grill. 'James will stay there for the present till he gets
somewhere of his own and Cathy will marry him in
the end.'

'Cathy?' she said. 'But they argue so much!'

'It's Cathy's way of doing things—blowing hot and
cold just for the devil of it, but she's grown up a lot in
the past few months, I think. She loved Amy on
sight, and through Amy she'll come to love Amy's
father.'

'How happy that makes me,' Margot was forced to
confess.

'Stay that way!' He kissed her once again. 'And
come back to Scotland with me in the morning.'

'I've wanted to do that ever since I left,' she
confessed, taking a moment to think about the
future. 'What about my father?' she asked.

'He'll stay at Ottershaws for a while longer, I
expect,' Elliott said. 'Until he sees James finally
settled with Cathy,' he added, 'and then he will be
off on his travels again.' He paused, still holding her
tightly. 'Don't try to hold him back, Margot,' he
added kindly. 'Let him go free, because that is what
he wants.'

'Did he know you were coming to look for me in
London?' she asked, piling the grilled bacon on to the
platter she had heated in the oven. 'Did he approve?'

'I think he did,' he answered quietly. 'Anyway, he
wished me luck.'

They retrieved the over-cooked bacon from the
oven, laughing at the disaster as they held each other
by the hand.

'I'll do better next time!' Margot promised.

'At Sun Hill,' he suggested. 'This place is really far
too small!'

'I'll never be able to forget it, all the same.' She put

her arms about his neck. 'Oh, Elliott, it's the one place I'll always remember, because you came to me here. How could I ever forget that?'

'I wouldn't ask you to try,' he said, 'although I'll make a shrewd guess that you might once you get back to Scotland.'

The following morning they drove back to London to return Henry's car.

'This is a surprise!' he exclaimed, showing them into his office. 'I didn't think you would come back so soon.'

There was a faint twinkle in his eyes as he waited for them to explain the urgency of their return.

'Henry, we're getting married,' Margot told him, clinging to Elliott's hand.

Henry took a long time to appreciate their news, while he considered the transformation it had wrought.

'I'm not going to say I'm *absolutely* delighted,' he confessed, 'because I'm also disappointed.'

'About my career?' Margot crossed to his side. 'Henry, I'm sorry!' she said.

'So am I.' He put an arm about her shoulders. 'Though you needn't give up entirely,' he suggested.

'One-night stands, Henry?' She shook her head. 'It's not what you wanted.'

'It would keep your hand—or rather, your voice in. They're not a bad thing now that I know America is out of the question,' he added, looking at Elliott.

'Margot must make up her own mind,' Elliott said. 'I won't stand in her way if she wants to sing.'

'I can do that in my bath! I already do, so be warned!' She smiled across the room at her future husband as she said goodbye to the man who had mapped out a great future for her.

'Give me a year or two,' she begged. 'After that—who knows?'

'I think I do,' Henry told her, saying goodbye to success. 'But off you go and get married and start raising a family. It will do you good!'

He walked with them to the door, a certain wistfulness in his eyes.

'Don't forget you can do two things equally well,' he pointed out as they turned away. 'A career and a marriage can easily go hand in hand if you work hard at them both.'

Margot put her hand in Elliott's as they walked slowly down the stairs.

'Our marriage must always come first,' she decided. 'Before everything.'

They took the train north two days later to find James waiting for them at Berwick with the Range Rover.

'Dad has the car,' he explained, helping them with their luggage. 'He's gone with Cathy to look at a house.'

'Whatever for?' Margot asked.

'To live in. Cathy has promised to marry me.'

They gazed at him in total surprise.

'So soon?' Margot said. 'We thought——'

'Apparently it's now or never,' he laughed, 'because this has always been the house she wanted. It's Eckersley,' he explained to Elliott, 'on the far side of the dale. It has a fair amount of grazing to offer, and it isn't too far away from the Mains. Dad will come with us,' he added, 'until he makes up his mind about what he wants to do, so it rather puts you in a spot as far as Ottershaws is concerned.'

'There isn't any problem,' Margot told him, holding fast to Elliott's hand. 'We'll be living there one day soon. You aren't the only person who's going to be married, Jamie,' she added quietly.

'Isn't Amy going to have a whale of a time being a bridesmaid twice!' Her brother laughed to cover his genuine surprise. 'But what about Sun Hill?' he asked after a moment. 'What will happen to it?'

'We'll keep it as a sort of bothy,' Elliott decided, turning to Margot. 'That's another new word for you,' he smiled, 'to add to factors and bannocks and curly kale!'

They went out of the station together for their first view of the Border hills.

'There's no reason why we shouldn't all be as happy as Larry here,' James declared, looking about him. 'It's the place to be!'

Cathy and Amy were waiting for them when they drew up at Ottershaws.

'We've got it!' Cathy cried, looking at James with starry eyes. 'We've got Eckersley, the house I've always wanted!'

'And I'm going to be bridesmaid,' Amy echoed. 'Won't that be nice?'

'I can't think of anything better,' Margot agreed, returning Elliott's smile.

HARLEQUIN
Romance

Coming Next Month

Available in June wherever paperback books are sold, or through Harlequin Reader Service:

In the U.S.
901 Fuhrmann Blvd.
P.O. Box 1397
Buffalo, N.Y. 14240-1397

In Canada
P.O. Box 603
Fort Erie, Ontario
L2A 5X3

HARLEQUIN
American Romance®

THE LOVES OF A CENTURY...

Join American Romance in a nostalgic look back at the Twentieth Century—at the lives and loves of American men and women from the turn-of-the-century to the dawn of the year 2000.

Journey through the decades from the dance halls of the 1900s to the discos of the seventies ... from Glenn Miller to the Beatles ... from Valentino to Newman ... from corset to miniskirt ... from beau to Significant Other.

Relive the moments ... recapture the memories.

Look for the CENTURY OF AMERICAN ROMANCE series starting next month in Harlequin American Romance. In one of the four American Romance titles appearing each month, for the next twelve months, we'll take you back to a decade of the Twentieth Century, where you'll relive the years and rekindle the romance of days gone by.

Don't miss a day of the CENTURY OF AMERICAN ROMANCE.

A CENTURY OF
AMERICAN ROMANCE
1900's

The women...the men...the passions...
the memories....